Wendy Orr

NIM'S ISLAND

illustrated by
Kerry Millard

SCHOLASTIC INC.

New York Toronto London Auckland Sydney
Mexico City New Delhi Hong Kong Buenos Aires

ISBN 0-439-37263-1

12 11 10 9 8 7 6 5 4 3 2   7/0

Printed in the U.S.A.   40

First Scholastic printing, October 2002

With thanks to my parents, who searched their logbooks and photograph albums to help build Nim's Island, and to all my family, friends, and Internet acquaintances who answered my requests for odd information on coconuts, whistling shells, and broken rudders.

W.O.

IN A PALM TREE, on an island, in the middle of the wide blue sea, was a girl.

Nim's hair was wild, her eyes were bright, and around her neck she wore three cords. One was for a spyglass, one for a whorly, whistling shell, and one for a fat red pocketknife in a sheath.

With the spyglass at her eye, she watched her father's boat. It sailed out through the reef to the deeper dark ocean, and Jack turned to wave and Nim waved back, though she knew he couldn't see.

Then the white sails caught the wind and blew him out of sight, and Nim was alone. For three days and three nights, whatever happened or needed doing, Nim would do it.

"And what we need first," said Nim, "is breakfast!" So she threw four ripe coconuts *thump!* into the sand and climbed down after them.

Then she whistled her shell, two long, shrill notes that carried far out to the reef, where the sea lions were fishing. Selkie popped her head above the water. She had a fish in her mouth, but she swallowed it fast and dived toward the beach.

And from a rock by the hut, Fred came scuttling. Fred was an iguana, spiky as a dragon, with a cheerful snub nose. He twined round Nim's feet in a prickly hug.

"Are you saying good morning," Nim demanded, "or just begging for breakfast?"

Fred stared at the coconuts. He was a very honest iguana.

Coconuts are tricky to open, but Nim was an expert. With a rock and a spike, she punched a hole and drank the juice, cracked the shell and pried out the flesh. Fred snatched his piece and gulped it down.

Marine iguanas don't eat coconut, but no one had ever told Fred.

Now Selkie was flopping up the beach to greet them. "We'll come in, too!" Nim shouted, and dived off the rocks.

Selkie twisted and shot up underneath, gliding Nim through the waves: thumping over, ducking under. Nim clung tight, till she was half sea lion and half girl, and all of her was part ocean.

Then Selkie and Fred went to sunbake on the rock and Nim went back to the hut. She poured a mug of water from her favorite blue bottle, brushed her teeth above a clump of grass that needed the spit, and started her chores. There were lots today, because she was doing some of Jack's as well as her own.

LONG AGO, when Nim was a baby, she'd had a mother as well as Jack. But one day, her mother had gone to investigate the contents of a blue whale's stomach. It was an interesting experiment that no one had done for thousands of years, and Jack said that it would have been all right, it should have been safe—until the Troppo Tourists came to make a film of it, shouting and racing their huge pink-and-purple boat around Nim's mother and the whale. When Jack told them to stop, they made rude signs and bumped their boat against the whale's nose.

The whale panicked and dived, so deep that no one ever knew where or when he came back up again.

Nim's mother never came back up at all.

So Jack packed his baby into his boat and sailed round and round the world, just in case Nim's mother came back up out of the ocean somewhere else and didn't know where to find them. Then one day, when the baby had grown into a very little girl, he'd found this island.

It was the most beautiful island in the whole world. It

N

E

W

S

Hissing
Stones

Keyhole
Cove

Sea Lion
Point

Lookout
Palm

Coral
Reef

Selkie's
Rock

Shell
Beach

Hut

Grasslands

Turtle
Beach

Ocean
Current

Not to Scale

had white shell beaches, pale gold sand, and tumbled black rocks where the spray threw rainbows into the sky. It had a fiery mountain with green rain forest on the high slopes and grasslands at the bottom. There was a pool of fresh water to drink and a waterfall to slide down, and, in a hidden hollow where the grasslands met the white shell beach, there was—"A place for a hut!"

And around it all, so that only the smallest boats could weave their way through, was a maze of reef, curving from the black rocks on one side to the white cliffs on the other.

Jack sailed back to a city for the very last time. He filled up the boat with plants for a garden and supplies for science, and he landed on the island to build a home for just him and his daughter, because he knew now that Nim's mother had stayed down at the bottom of the sea.

Like a mermaid, Nim thought.

He built a hut of driftwood logs and good strong branches, with a palm-thatched roof and a hard dirt floor. He put up a satellite dish, and a solar panel to charge the batteries for a flashlight, a cell phone, and a laptop computer.

He made sleeping mats stuffed with rustling palm fronds, a table and two stools, a desk, bookcases and shelves for his science stuff, coconut-shell bowls, and seashell plates. He dug a vegetable garden in the rich soil at Fire Mountain's base and planted avocados, bananas, lettuce, oranges, pineapples, strawberries, sweet potatoes, and tomatoes, and bamboo for making pipes and useful things.

Then he went on being a scientist, and when Nim got older, she helped him. They read what the barometer said, measured how much rain fell every day and how strong the winds were, how high the high tides reached and how low the low tides fell, and then they marked the measurements on a clean white chart with a dark blue marker.

They studied the plants that grew on the island and the animals that lived there. They put blue bands on the birds' legs and wrote down the numbers so Jack could remember the birds' birthdays and who their mothers and fathers were. (Nim remembered anyway.)

Sometimes Jack wrote articles about the weather and the plants and animals, and e-mailed them to science magazines and universities, and sometimes people e-mailed him questions to answer. He would tell them about tropical storms and iguanas and seaweed, but he would never tell them where the island was, in case the Troppo Tourists ever found it, because Jack hated the Troppo Tourists worse than sea snakes or scorpions. Only

the supply ship—which came once a year to bring them books and paper, flour and yeast, nails and cloth, and the other things they couldn't make themselves—knew where they lived. It was too big to weave its way through the reef, so Jack and Nim always sailed out to meet it, and the ship's captain never saw just how beautiful the island was.

And every day, no matter how excited Jack got about finding a new kind of seashell or butterfly, they looked after their garden; they watered it if it was dry, weeded the weeds, and picked what was ripe. Jack built a three-sided

shed for the tools, with a hook for the bananas and his big machete to cut them with. The machete was Nim's favorite tool.

When they'd looked after the garden and fished for dinner and checked the beaches for driftwood or bottles or anything else that might have floated in on the tide, Nim had school.

That was what they called it, but it wasn't inside and it wasn't at a desk. They sat on the beach in the dark to study the stars, and climbed cliffs to see birds in their nests. Nim learned the language of dolphins, about the tiny crabs that float out to sea on their coconut homes, and how to watch the clouds and listen to the wind.

Sometimes for a whole day they talked in sea lion grunts or frigate bird squawks or plankton wiggles.

Jack loved plankton. Nim's favorites were the ones that shone bright in the sea at night, but Jack loved them all because they were so little, and so important because little fish ate them, and bigger fish ate the little fish, and the biggest fish ate the bigger fish, and there wouldn't have been any fish at all if it weren't for plankton.

But Nim liked animals that you could see, and have fun with, so when Jack had said he was going sailing for three days to collect plankton, Nim had decided to stay home.

"I'll phone every night at sunset," said Jack. "And then you can check the e-mail. If you don't hear from me or see me for three days, send an SOS."

But Nim knew that Jack would be okay because he was the best sailor on the ocean, and Jack knew that Nim would be okay because Selkie was always with her (Selkie sometimes forgot that Nim was strong and smart, and looked after her as if she were a tiny pup).

Even when the king of the sea lions barked at her to come and fish or snuggle down at night with her sea lion family, Selkie stayed close to Nim.

2

ALL THAT FIRST day alone Nim did the things that she did when Jack was home. Sometimes she even forgot that he wasn't just somewhere else on the island, measuring the bubbles at the Hissing Stones or counting eggs in a kittiwake's nest.

But when she went to bed, the wind began to blow.

It had been the tiniest breeze as she sat on the beach to watch the sun go down and wait for the phone to ring; the barest stirring of the palms as Jack said hello.

"Did you find interesting plankton?" she asked.

"Millions," said Jack. "Trillions. And some greedy birds who thought I was fishing."

"Faraway birds?"

"Home birds. The big one you call Galileo swooped me in case my microscope was a fish. I told him to go home and bother you."

Nim laughed. "He did! I only caught one fish all afternoon—and he snitched it right out of my hand! So I gave up and read on Selkie's Rock."

"Good book?"

"*Mountain Madness.* You said it was your very favorite, remember?"

"So I did," said Jack.

"Because it's exciting?"

"I liked the people in it," said Jack. "I felt as if the hero could be my friend."

"It'd be funny having a friend that could talk."

"Honk, whuffle, grunt," said Jack in his best sea lion voice. "Selkie can talk! She's just not very good at telling stories."

Nim patted Selkie in case that hurt her feelings.

"Don't forget to check the e-mail," Jack went on. "Say I'll answer in a few days. Unless it's the Troppo Tourists—I'd rather meet six hungry sharks than that pink-and-purple boat!"

"I'd rather meet a cyclone at sea!"

"I'd rather jump in the fire from Fire Mountain . . . or talk to Nim when she hasn't had enough sleep!" said Jack. "Don't stay up too late reading!"

So Nim blew iguana kisses into the phone and went back to the hut, and the breeze flicked her hair and was cool against her cheek.

It was already dark in the hut, and when she checked the e-mail, even though she didn't know anyone in the wide, wide world who might send her a letter, it made her lonely to see "No Messages" in the e-mail box on the screen.

"Good night, Selkie!" Nim called. "Good night, Fred!"

Fred was already asleep in his little rock cave beside the hut, but there was a quiet honk from Selkie's Rock.

Nim lay down on her mat with her flashlight and her book. The waves rumbled onto the reef and mumbled across the sand. The breeze whistled through the cracks in the walls, and there was no comforting noise of Jack humming to himself or turning pages.

Nim felt excited and brave and a tiny bit afraid, but the second chapter of *Mountain Madness* was even more exciting than the first, and she thought about the hero till she went to sleep.

The wind grew stronger. It howled at the door and screamed through the windows; it laughed at Nim because Jack wasn't there, and she didn't know if it was just teasing her or was going to grow to a tree-throwing, hut-smashing storm.

She switched on the flashlight and crept outside.

The clouds were scudding across the moon; the stars had disappeared and there was a lashing of rain. Nim stumbled and nearly dropped her flashlight, but she could see Selkie's shape, darker than the night, and heard her bark, deeper than the wind.

Selkie nuzzled Nim's shoulder and curled tight around her. The wind passed, the tail of a storm roaring out to sea, and Nim was snug in her sea lion shelter, breathing the warm smell of fur.

Next morning, coconuts were scattered over the beach and the hut had a dent in the roof, but the solar panel was safe and the satellite dish, sitting above the hut like a fat white coconut, was still waiting for messages to bounce across the world and into Jack's e-mail.

Inside, the hut was gritty with sand. *Mountain Madness* had blown open, and a piece of newspaper Jack had used as a bookmark was stuck against a wall. Nim tucked it back inside the cover and started cleaning the hut.

She shook her sleeping mat outside the door, swept out the sand, and used a scrap of old T-shirt to dust the laptop and Jack's science stuff, her polished driftwood, a threaded wreath of shells, and the picture of her mother.

Her mother had bright, clever eyes and a wide, funny smile; she looked happy-excited because it was the morning she went diving to investigate the contents of the blue whale's stomach.

Nim put the photo back on the shelf.

She put her empty water bottles into her wagon and

whistled for Fred—Fred liked going wherever Nim went, especially places where Selkie couldn't follow. He curled spikily around her neck and they towed the wagon across the grassland, up to the tangled vines and ferns of the rain forest.

At the edge of the rain forest was a wide rock pool with a waterfall tumbling into it, and on the other side of the pool was the garden.

There were plants to prop up that had toppled over in the wind, weeds to pull, strawberries to nibble, and a huge bunch of bananas just green enough to pick.

Nim liked bananas, but what she liked even better was swinging Jack's machete. It was shiny and sharp and made her feel like a pirate.

"Aargh, me hearties!" she shouted, and chopped down the bunch.

She dragged them to the shed and hooked them to a rope looping over a beam in the roof.

"I'm swinging the bananas!" And she grabbed the rope just above her head. Fred jumped and clung to the end with his claws. Swinging hard and heavy, they hoisted the bananas up to the roof to ripen.

It would have been easier if Selkie had helped, but sea lions aren't much good at swinging on ropes.

Nim put the machete away. "Are you hot?"

Fred knew what she was thinking. He raced her up the path to the top of the waterfall.

Over thousands of years, the water trickling down the mountain had worn away the steep black rocks to make a curving slide. It was perfect for *whoosh*ing a girl and an iguana over bumps and dips and splashing them into the pool at the bottom.

Nim and Fred ran up and slid down until it was time for lunch. Then Nim picked up a tomato and an avocado that had fallen off in the wind and weeded quickly around the peas.

"They'll be ready tomorrow," she told Fred.

But Fred didn't like peas, and he was getting bored. He started chewing leaves and spitting them out.

"I won't bring you up to the garden again!" Nim said sternly. Fred spat out the last bit of pea leaf and crawled into the wagon for a wild ride down the hill.

THAT NIGHT, when she sat on the rocks with the phone and watched the sun sink red into the waters, Jack didn't call. She pressed his number, but his phone didn't ring and he didn't answer.

She checked the e-mail and there was nothing there, either.

Nightmare pictures sneaked into Nim's head: upside-down boats, sinking boats, boats sailing off into the distance with fallen-off people swimming behind ...

She pushed the scenes away angrily. Jack was busy. He was concentrating on his plankton and didn't know what time it was—like when he was doing science things at home and forgot to eat.

She picked up her book, and soon she wasn't Nim anymore, she was a strong, brave hero scrambling up a cliff, she was swinging across a chasm, reaching for the other side ... and rubbing her aching eyes, looking up to see that the hut was dark and her flashlight beam was fading into the night. But she stayed being a hero till she went to sleep, because tonight she liked it better than being Nim.

3

WHEN THE SUN rose pink over Fire Mountain, Nim phoned Jack again, but there was still no answer; no ring; nothing at all.

Nim checked the phone…the satellite dish…the connections between the solar panel and the phone's battery charger…

But everything looked the way it should.

She checked her e-mail, even though she knew he didn't have a computer on his boat.

To: jack.rusoe@explorer.net
From: aka@incognito.net
Date: Tuesday 30 March, 22:21
Dear Jack Rusoe,
    Your article "The Life Cycle of the Coconut Palm" was as fascinating as a feature film and as fact-filled as a documentary! But I still have a couple of questions…
    1) How long do coconuts float?
    2) Do they float well enough to make a raft?
    3) How could I build one?
Thank you, Alex Rover

"A letter!" said Nim.

She knew it wasn't hers; she knew that Alex Rover was just asking Jack a science question—but it was still a letter. It was as if someone, somewhere in the world, knew she was alone and was saying hello.

To: aka@incognito.net
From: jack.rusoe@explorer.net
Date: Wednesday 31 March, 6:45
Dear Alex Rover,
    Jack is busy doing science. I hope he will answer your questions tomorrow or maybe the day after.
From Nim

She had heaps to do, and that was good because she didn't want time to worry about Jack.

She made banana-and-coconut mush and snuggled warmly with Selkie to eat it for breakfast. Fred always forgot that he didn't like bananas, so he snitched a bit from her bowl and spat it out across the rock.

"Yuck, Fred!" said Nim. She didn't feel much like eating now, either.

She watered her garden with bamboo pipes trickling coolly from the pool. She towed wagonloads of seaweed to spread around the plants. She picked ten ripe strawberries and a handful of peas.

Jack loved strawberries.

She made
a new broom
with a fallen-
down palm branch
and swept the hut again.
She filled in Jack's charts with a big NO
across the space for rain, and the
numbers for barometric pressure and sea
temperature, and EAST for where the wind was
coming from. She wished it would turn around
and blow Jack home, and she climbed the tall
palm tree just in case she could see the white
sails. And when she couldn't, her stomach tied
itself into a hard, tight knot, and she went on
being busy. She mixed up dough to make some
bread. It grew swollen and puffy and she punched it
hard in the middle, *oof*ing the air out of the puffiness
and the knot out of herself. She punched and rolled
it, over and over, till her arms were floppy and the
doughball was smooth. Then she wrapped it in a fresh
banana leaf and carried it to the Hissing Stones, where
Fire Mountain met the rocks of Keyhole Cove, and
fountains of steamy water sometimes shot high and wild
into the air.

Today there was just the small yellow pool splattering
slimy bubbles, and the rocks around—too hot to touch,

24

hissing steam from every crack. And the smell, like a rotten frigate bird's egg smashed on the beach.

Nim squatted at the edge, out of the way of the wind and stink. She shaped her dough into eight flat pancakes and flicked them one by one onto the hot rock.

What Nim liked best about cooking bread was watching the dough she'd mixed from dry flour, yeast, and water puff into warm, fresh bread. "Science," Jack said, but Nim thought it was magic.

Today it was nothing.

Today, when the bread bubbled and puffed in the middle, it didn't even make her smile. When she flipped it over with her bamboo flipping stick and then neatly back into her banana leaf, it was just bread, because cooking bread was what she had to do today. And if she did everything that she was supposed to, then Jack would come home tonight and everything would be all right.

So she went on doing jobs, busy busy busy all day. She heaped fallen branches into a bonfire; beachcombed from the Black Rocks of Keyhole Cove to Shell Beach in front of the hut, and then from the sands of Turtle Beach right to the Frigate Bird Cliffs at the end. (And she found three giant seeds shaped like hearts, ten new seashells, and half a wooden paddle that made her think, Oh, no! But it wasn't Jack's.) Suddenly she was too tired to do anything more. She made a banana sandwich and curled up on the rock between Selkie and Fred to read the last chapter of her book.

When she finished, she felt happy and sad at the same time, because the ending was warm and smiley but she didn't want to say good-bye to the people in the book.

"I'll read it again!" Nim decided, and read the title out loud, as if she'd never seen it before: "*Mountain Madness,* by Alex Rover.

"Alex Rover!" she shouted.

Fred fell off the rock and Selkie honked crossly at being woken from her nap. "Sorry," said Nim.

She opened the book again and unfolded the newspaper bookmark.

ALEX ROVER—AUTHOR OR HERO?

The most famous writer in the world has written a new book: Mountain Madness *(Papyrus Publishing, $15.95).*

Cliff-hanging adventure, romantic love story—read it and you'll think you're living it! You'll feel the cold rush of wind as you jump out of a plane, the sweat on your palms as you rappel down a cliff.

So, is Alex Rover the author—or the hero?

He couldn't describe these adventures if he hadn't lived them. But Alex Rover is not a typical macho action-man.

Anyone lucky enough to meet him will find a very special human being—a mountain climber who finds poetry on the peak, an explorer who sings the glories of the stars.

Unfortunately, meeting him is not easy to do. He refuses to give interviews or photographs. Delia Defoe, his editor at Papyrus Publishing, claims that she has never met him—or even spoken to him on the phone!

"We correspond by e-mail," she says.

"We correspond by e-mail," Nim repeated. It sounded important and funny. "I correspond with Alex Rover by e-mail.

"Selkie," she said, "Alex Rover's a hero.

"Fred," she added, "I *correspond* with a hero."

Selkie and Fred looked confused. They liked it when Nim used words they knew, like *coconut* and *fish*, *swimming* and *Keyhole Cove*.

But Nim was happy. If Alex Rover could survive all those wonderful adventures, so could Jack. He'd be home tomorrow, just like he said.

To: aka@incognito.net
From: jack.rusoe@explorer.net
Date: Wednesday 31 March, 18:27
Dear Alex Rover,
    Jack is still away, but I hope he'll be home soon. I'm glad you're a hero because **Mountain Madness** is the best book I've ever read. It's like real life except more exciting and everyone is so brave. And because it has a happy ending when the hero and the lady find each other and fall in love.
From Nim

To: jack.rusoe@explorer.net
From: aka@incognito.net
Date: Wednesday 31 March, 13:32
Dear Nim,

Aren't time differences funny? When it's nighttime where I live, the sun's coming up for you. You're living in my tomorrow!

The other funny thought is me being a hero—I'm as un-hero as anyone can be!

I can climb mountains if they're made out of paper, and swim rivers if they're in my bathtub (with lots of bubble bath)...

I'm not even brave enough to talk to reporters. That's why they make up stories about me—one reporter even made up my name, and called me Alexander!!

Yours, Alex (Alexandra!) Rover

Nim had never heard the name Alexandra.

Alex Rover had never thought that anyone could be all alone on a tiny island in the middle of the ocean.

And so Nim went on thinking that Alex Rover was a man, and Alex went on thinking that Nim was a girl at home with her mother and maybe brothers and sisters, cousins and friends. And they both thought that they understood each other perfectly.

FAR, FAR OUT in the ocean, a sailboat drifted. On its deck, a man lay sprawled like a boxer who'd lost a fight.

28

A frigate bird, his dark wings as wide as the man was tall, swooped curiously.

Jack opened his eyes. He was hot, thirsty, and sore all over. When he scratched his beard, his hand came back rusty with dry blood.

He sat up and remembered.

He'd been sitting on the deck, watching the plankton glow on the nighttime waves. Suddenly a storm had come roaring, and he'd pulled down the sails, but the wind didn't care. It threw the boat sideways and he'd reached for the satellite dish as it smashed to the deck.

Now there was a cut on his head and the satellite dish was gone. And if the satellite dish was gone, his phone wouldn't work, and he must go home to Nim.

Jack's head hurt and his legs wobbled, but he staggered to the tiller. He pushed the tiller and then he pulled it, but it swung loose and empty in his hand and he knew his rudder was broken. If his rudder was broken, then he couldn't steer.

And if he couldn't steer, his boat was just a big piece of driftwood.

4

AT KEYHOLE COVE, the reef met the rocks in a huge ring. On one side were the worn gray rocks where the sea lions sat, and on the other the harsh black rocks of the wild east coast.

Inside the ring, the water was calm and a light, clear blue. The sea shushed in and out through a hole in the reef, but only the biggest waves could break over the top.

It was a perfect place for swimming. You could float on your back because if you started to daydream you'd bump your head on the reef before you floated out to sea. When you rolled over, you could watch sea horses and shells and the open jaws of the giant clams with polka-dot fish racing through them.

It was the perfect place to do a coconut experiment and find out how to make a raft for Alex Rover.

So early next morning, Nim loaded up her wagon with coconuts. Fred climbed on top and she towed them across the grasslands (because it was easier than towing a wagon across sand and rocks) to Keyhole Cove.

Selkie swam around to Sea Lion Point and sat and barked for Nim to hurry up.

But Nim got another load and then another, till she had twenty fat coconuts heaped on the rocks, and then she hurled them into the water one by one.

The coconuts bombed in and bobbed up. Selkie barked louder and louder. Fred got so excited he dived in with the last one.

Nim and Selkie jumped in, too. There was still lots of room in the cove, even with twenty floating coconuts. Lots of room for Nim to float and somersault and stand on her hands, and for Fred to dash and dive and for Selkie to *swish splash* the water through the Keyhole Rock.

When Selkie was bored with splashing, she grabbed Fred by the tail. It was Selkie's favorite game, but she was so big and Fred was so little that it really wasn't fair. Fred's legs whirred—he paddled faster and faster, harder and harder—but he couldn't get anywhere.

"Leave him alone, Selkie!" Nim shouted. But it was hard not to laugh, and Fred sulked at the bottom of the cove when Selkie finally let him go.

JUST BEFORE SUNSET, Nim tried to phone Jack again—just in case he'd forgotten; just in case his phone had been broken and now it was fixed—but there was no answer.

It was two days since he'd phoned. If he didn't come home tomorrow, she could send an SOS: *Go and Find Jack!*

But Jack wouldn't want help and she didn't want to send it.

She walked up to the pool to fill her water bottle and pick more peas for dinner. He'll be home in the morning, she thought. Something will happen!

And something did.

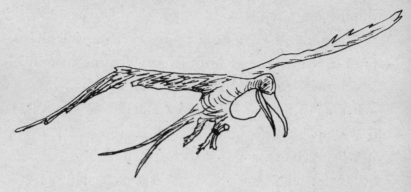

A frigate bird dived to scoop a drink from the pool. Sticking out from his leg band was a rolled-up piece of paper.

It was easy to call Galileo if you had a fish, but Nim didn't. "Come here," she coaxed. "Come to me."

The big bird teased and soared, turned and dived. He swooped over Nim, so low that his wings brushed her hair, and so slowly that she could pull the letter out of the band.

Dear Nim,

I figure if I offer Galileo a fish he'll let me post this letter to you.

Had a fight with a freak storm. Storm won. Took my satellite dish, a bit of my rudder, and a chunk of my forehead.

Can't figure out if I've slept for one day or two. Don't send an SOS—it'll take more than a broken rudder to stop me from getting home!

Love (as much as a frigate bird loves fish),

Jack

Nim ran all the way down the hill, waving the letter in one hand and the water bottle in the other. "Jack's okay!" she sang, and swung Fred in a crazy jig around Selkie. "He'll be home soon!"

Then she wrote two letters.

Dear Jack,

I was SO HAPPY when Galileo gave me your letter. I didn't really think you'd forget to come home, but I liked that better than some of the other ideas.

I've been very busy doing an experiment, but I'll tell you about it when you get home because I have to write an e-mail now.

Love (as much as Fred loves coconut),

Nim

To: aka@incognito.net
From: jack.rusoe@explorer.net
Date: Thursday 1 April, 18:30
Dear Alex Rover,

Today I started an experiment to find out how you could build your raft.

I dropped twenty coconuts into Keyhole Cove to see how long they'll float. They won't escape unless there's a bad storm with really big waves.

I hope there won't be.
From Nim

She peeled a banana, dropped it onto a piece of bread, and sprinkled it with fresh seaweed.

"1 message," said the e-mail box on the screen.

To: jack.rusoe@explorer.net
From: aka@incognito.net
Date: Thursday 1 April, 13:37
Dear Nim,

My hero would be devastated, annihilated, depressed, and soggy if his raft didn't float!

What does Keyhole Cove look like?

I picture a ring of black rocks jutting out from the shore, stark against the blue sea—and bobbing ridiculously around in this idyllic pool, twenty coconuts waiting to be a raft.

The Coconuts of Keyhole Cove—sounds like a title! Hmm...
With a thousand thanks, Alex

Nim read the letter three times. It made her feel warm and smiley, like finishing *Mountain Madness*—and when Alex Rover described Keyhole Cove, it was as if he knew the island, and Nim, too.

5

NIM STOOD IN the doorway, looking out to sea one last time before the sun set, just in case Jack got home faster than he thought, because no matter how much she liked reading letters from Alex Rover, she'd like to see Jack's sails even more.

Through the shadows she could see not a boat, but a browny-green dot floating in on the waves.

"Chica's coming!" Nim shouted, but Selkie and Fred had settled down for the night; Selkie grumble-barked, but neither of them moved.

In a few minutes, it would be completely dark. Nim pulled on her sweater and grabbed the flashlight.

Its light shone pale in the dusk as she jumped down the rocks to Turtle Beach. Walking slowly on the cold night sand, she turned off the flashlight and waited.

The turtle paddled steadily toward her, a hump of shell glooming dark in the gray waves, and heaved herself onto the sand.

Nim crept closer. "Welcome home, Chica!"

Chica was too busy to answer. She dragged her huge body up above the reach of the highest tide and started scooping out sand with her strong front flippers. It was hard, grunting work.

Nim squatted beside her, watching quietly in the darkness and wiping away sand from the turtle's watery eyes, until the hole was just as deep and wide as it needed to be.

The stars scattered brightly and were mirrored in the sea, a fat crescent moon rose amongst them, and egg after round white egg rolled into the bottom of the nest.

"Ninety-nine!" Nim whispered as Chica pushed sand back into the hole, rocking her heavy body back and forth till the sand was thumped hard and smooth. She didn't want anyone else to know where her precious babies were hidden.

"Maybe in a few years," Nim told her, "ninety-nine turtles will come back and lay their eggs here, too!"

For as long as she could remember, Chica had been the only turtle to swim out of the sea, back to this beach where she was hatched, to lay her own eggs.

"But maybe this year some of your daughters will be old enough." She tickled Chica's wrinkly chin till her wise turtle eyes blinked with happiness. "You can meet them when they come to lay their eggs—and then their daughters will come back, and then their daughters, and there'll be lots of turtles again!"

Chica blinked again, sleepily this time.

Nim kissed the top of her leathery head and followed the flashlight beam back to her own bed.

JACK DIDN'T KNOW why Chica liked to stay instead of leaving as soon as her eggs were laid, the way sea turtles were supposed to. Nim knew. Chica liked visiting her friends.

She showed it in the way she rubbed her throat across Fred's spiky back, let Selkie sniff her nose, and let Nim tickle her chin. She showed it in the way she nodded and blinked as Nim wondered about the places she'd been and what she'd seen, and told her what they'd been doing, and about Jack's broken rudder and Alex Rover's letters. Chica wasn't cuddly, but she was a good listener.

As the morning got hotter, they lazed in the calm shallows off Turtle Beach. Chica was tired because she'd swum hundreds of kilometers and laid ninety-nine eggs. Nim was tired because she'd stayed up so late watching Chica lay eggs. Selkie was tired because she'd worried about Nim staying up so late. Fred wasn't tired, but he didn't mind being lazy if everyone else was.

Just before sunset, Nim raced up to the vegetable garden to see what was ripe. She picked a lettuce and a tomato for a salad and dug up a sweet potato to bake in a celebration bonfire, with fresh limpets from the rocks and coconut for dessert.

To: aka@incognito.net
From: jack.rusoe@explorer.net
Date: Friday 2 April, 18:25
Dear Alex Rover,

   I didn't check the coconut experiment today because last night Chica came onto Turtle Beach to lay her eggs, and she likes me to sit with her while she does it. Chica is a green turtle, and she likes Selkie and Fred, too, so we spent nearly the whole day with her.

   Jack will be home soon, too, and he can check if I'm doing the experiment the right way.
From Nim
P.S. Keyhole Cove is just like you described it!

To: jack.rusoe@explorer.net
From: aka@incognito.net
Date: Friday 2 April, 13:30
Dear Nim,

I think the right way to do the experiment is any way my chief experimenter wants to!

Now I'm imagining Turtle Beach: pale gold sands marked by the flipper prints of a very special turtle! And your footprints beside her prints...

I'm turtle green with envy!

Yours, Alex

ALEX ROVER SAT and stared at her computer. It wasn't easy to see because the desk was stacked with books about oceans and islands; magazines about boats and rafts; videos about seabirds and animals.

The walls were covered by a map of the world; charts of the moon and stars; paintings of the sea: calm and blue, wild and gray, and every other mood between; and pictures of sandy beaches, rocky cliffs, coconut trees, tropical islands, coral reefs, seagulls, and frigate birds.

But Alex was thinking about Nim and wondering whether Selkie and Fred were her sister and brother, or pets.

NIM WOKE UP thinking about Alex Rover's raft.

You can't hammer two coconuts together, she decided, but if I had a thin piece of board...and lined the coconuts in rows...I could hammer a nail through the board and into the coconuts.

But coconuts are hard to hold still while you hammer. They roll around so that sometimes you hit the wrong thing..."Ouch!" Nim yelled—so loud and so often that Fred went to sulk in his cave in case it was his fault.

After two hours, she had a black-and-blue thumb and a pile of coconut for lunch. And one unsmashed coconut. "Let's go and see Chica!" said Nim.

Chica was resting on the damp sand watching the tide go out. She blinked happily when she saw what her friends were carrying.

Chica's favorite game was coconut soccer.

That was what Nim called it, because soccer was the only ball game she'd seen a picture of—and because nobody else has ever thought of a name for a game with a girl, a sea lion, a turtle, and an iguana all trying to be the first to get a floating coconut to shore. There were no rules except that Selkie wasn't supposed to pull Fred's tail and Chica wasn't supposed to sit on the coconut underwater.

Selkie cheated a lot; Chica didn't cheat much, but when she did, she was very good at it.

So Nim threw the coconut into the water, and Fred dashed at it because he was the fastest and best at guessing where it would land, and Selkie sneaked under him and splashed the nut across the sea. Then she tried to throw Fred across the sea, too, but Nim saw her and shouted, and while Selkie was trying to look innocent, Chica grabbed the coconut.

She tucked it tight under her strong turtle chin and didn't even notice everyone tickling and pulling, wrestling and shoving. She towed them all toward the beach, and when she got to the edge of the water, she sank to the bottom with the coconut under her and wouldn't move. And since no one could move Chica if she didn't want them to, that was the end of the game.

"It's a tie," said Nim. "Chica can't say she's won if the coconut's still in the water, so it's zero-all."

Chica looked as smug as a green turtle can look, and didn't seem to mind at all.

LATE IN THE afternoon, Nim walked around to Keyhole Cove to check the coconuts. All twenty were still bobbing cheerfully around the cove, bumping and floating, loose and free ...

"I've got it!" Nim shouted.

To: aka@incognito.net
From: jack.rusoe@explorer.net
Date: Saturday 3 April, 18:20
Dear Alex Rover,

I've been thinking about how you would make a raft.

Hammering coconuts onto a board doesn't work because the shell breaks, and if it didn't break right away, I think bits of it would fall off later and then the raft might sink.

What if you put the coconuts in a sort of bag? How would you make the bag?

Where are you going on your raft?
From Nim

To: jack.rusoe@explorer.net
From: aka@incognito.net
Date: Saturday 3 April, 13:23
Dear Nim,

I feel like a queen bee, lazing while you buzz!

A bag raft sounds perfect. Now I just need a reason for my hero to find a large sack on a deserted tropical island! Or maybe the bad guys stick him in a sack when they throw him overboard! As long as they don't tie it up too well.

My hero's going to a tiny Pacific island, where,

44

faster than a shopper at a half-price sale, he'll set off again to rescue the lady hero. (I'll be sitting at home, snug as a snail in its shell!)

I've attached a map I've drawn for the story—click on the icon.

With best wishes, Alex

Nim clicked.

Her stomach somersaulted.

She stared at the map on the wall and the map on the screen and the map on the wall again.

Jack liked maps; he drew maps of their island, the currents around it, and the places where they'd sailed. And because their island wasn't on the big map of the world, he'd drawn it on that, too, near the crossing of two lines—the one going around the world's middle like a belt, and an up-and-down line curving with the shape of the earth.

"This is the hero's island," Nim whispered. And that must mean...

"Selkie! Fred!" she shouted. "Alex Rover's been to our island!"

"I think," she added, a little while later.

It took a long time to go to sleep that night.

NEXT MORNING Nim sang her way through the weeding,

the digging, and the picking. She hummed as she measured and marked her charts, and she sang so loudly when she climbed Lookout Palm to check for sails that a seagull dropped his fish.

"That's what we'll do today!" said Nim, and slid down the tree.

She got her fishing rod and met Fred and Selkie at Turtle Beach. Chica was grazing the seaweed just where the water started to get deep. Selkie didn't like Nim to swim out deep, but she let her dive and visit for just a minute.

Fred stayed with Chica to see if she'd find an interesting sea plant he'd never eaten before; Selkie chased Nim back and went out deeper to fish; and Nim climbed up the rocks where she'd left her rod.

The rod was bamboo, strong and springy. Jack had made it for her birthday and taught her to cast the line in a whistling arc—the best part of fishing, Nim thought.

That was why she hated getting a fish first go: it was like finishing a ball game after one catch. Seven tries this

time, and then a fish dancing silver on the end of her line. It was a good one to eat, the right size ... "Sorry, fish," said Nim, and killed it quickly. That was the part she didn't like.

Selkie did, though. No matter how far away or how deep she was swimming, she always knew the instant that Nim had caught something.

"Wait!" Nim ordered, but it was hard for Selkie to be patient when fish were being cleaned and she was waiting for the guts and bits that Nim didn't want.

When the fish was cleaned and Selkie had stopped barking for more, Nim wrapped it in leaves and built a bonfire on the beach.

She dragged some fallen-down branches and driftwood into a pile and used dried palm leaves for kindling.

When Nim and Jack had a fire at night, they used matches, but matches were precious because they came on the supply ship, so in the daytime they used glass and the sun's own fire.

She unscrewed the lens from her spyglass. She pointed it so that the sun shone a bright beam on her kindling. A brown patch grew and glowed, and a small flame sparkled on the dry palm fronds, caught the small branches, and began to roar.

Then she dropped a sweet potato into the hot coals and toasted her fish on a long stick.

After lunch they all lay on the edge of the beach. The tide rippled over them, and when it started to float them away, they moved farther up. Nim got a book and read with her legs in the water and the rest of her on the sand.

And every few minutes she looked up to watch for sails and wait for e-mail time.

To: aka@incognito.net
From: jack.rusoe@explorer.net
Date: Sunday 4 April, 18:26
Dear Alex Rover,
    I have never been so excited in my WHOLE LIFE! (At least not since Fred learned to climb on my shoulders when I whistled.)
    Are you really the hero and have you been to our island? Because your map is exactly like our map and your hero's island is exactly where our island is. Is that how you knew what Keyhole Cove looked like, and

Turtle Beach?

Are you going to come back?

From Nim

To: jack.rusoe@explorer.net
From: aka@incognito.net
Date: Sunday 4 April, 13:29
Dear Nim,

This is as crazy-wonderful as—well, I can't think of anything as crazy-wonderful as an author making up an island and then e-mailing someone who lives there!

I'll tell you how it happened.

I made up a story about a brave hero and beautiful lady hero who sail around the world doing good things for science. To make the story exciting, I made up some bad guys who stole the boat, kidnapped the lady hero, and threw the hero overboard. But because the story needs a happy ending, I made up an island for him to land on, where he could build a raft and sail after the bad guys to rescue the lady hero.

So I looked on a map, and I made a dot where there was an ocean current to help drift him to the island, where the weather was warm enough for coconuts to grow, and where it seemed like a good place for a volcano to have grown into an island, long ago.

Will you be my island eyes and tell me what you see? Because I haven't been there, Nim, and I'm not hero enough to ever go.

All the best, Alex

7

FROM THE TOP of Fire Mountain, you could feel like a frigate bird, floating strong on the winds and seeing everywhere you wanted to see.

You could see the island's shores and beaches, and the grasslands and the cliffs and the rocks and the forest.

You could see far, far over the sea, every way that it rolled to the ends of the earth.

Early next morning, Nim whistled for Fred and hugged Selkie good-bye. "I'll be careful," she promised.

Then she checked that her spyglass was around her neck, to look for Jack; dropped a notebook and pencil in her pocket, to write things down for Alex; and packed two bananas, a piece of coconut, a pancake bread, and her bamboo cup into her backpack for a picnic along the way.

And she set off to climb Fire Mountain.

She stopped at the pool to fill her cup and shoved its bamboo lid back on tight, then climbed on up, past the top of the waterfall, following the creek through tangling vines and fly-munching flowers. The air steamed and sweat dribbled. "Get down and walk, Fred!" said Nim.

But Fred liked being carried, and he sprayed a cool saltwater sneeze across her neck.

"Okay," she said. "But we'll stop for a rest."

The creek was shallow and warm, but they flopped in, and it trickled over their hot bodies. Nim lay on her back and peeled a banana; Fred stared at the coconut.

"Later," said Nim.

Fred tried to sulk but was too hot to bother.

They climbed higher and the ground was gravelly and black; the plants were gray spikes and the creek disappeared.

Then there were no plants at all; just bubbling steam and the rotten-egg smell of the Hissing Stones, but a hundred times stronger.

"Pee-uh!" Nim coughed, and Fred sneezed a pathetic spray.

Long, long ago, the top of Fire Mountain had been a round green peak. Then, one rumbling, earthshaking day, it had poured out its heart of boiling, rolling, melting lava, and the round green peak had been blown away.

Now the top of the mountain was a sharp gray point, with a great smoky crater yawning below.

Nim wanted to look down into the crater, but the cloud of steam was too thick to see through and too choking to breathe. And the longer she stood on the rocks, the hotter they got, so she had to hop on one foot and then on the other, and then she had to run out of the smoke and away from the heat to the very top of the mountain.

She sat down and Fred climbed off her shoulders and they both took a deep breath.

"Picnic?" asked Nim, and they shared the coconut and the water. Then Nim ate her bread and her other banana and looked all around.

No matter which way or how far her spyglass stared, the ocean was empty. There were no white sails or anything else that could be Jack's boat. Nothing but a frigate bird, winging steadily out to the western sea. Maybe he'll bring me another message, thought Nim.

But first she was going to be Alex's island eyes.

Far below her was the top of Frigate Bird Cliffs; then Turtle Beach's pale gold sand, the grasslands and Shell Beach, and the hut; on to Sea Lion Point and Keyhole Cove; and finally the grim black lava rock that stretched all the way back to the far edge of Frigate Bird Cliffs. The island was built in layers, Nim thought: beach and rock, grassland and rain forest, and, last of all, the rocky Fire Mountain cone.

She picked up her notebook and pencil—but before she could start to write, the ground began to tremble.

Then the earth roared and the mountain bellowed and an explosion of red covered the sky. A fountain of lava,

red and
bubbling,
shot up
from the middle
of the crater. Red
and gold stars, hot and
boiling, sprayed over the
mountaintop.

It was like the wildest storm, when
wind and rain crash and great surf waves
thunder, except that the wind, the rain, and
the waves were all made of fire.

Fred was a streak of gray flying over gray
rocks, and Nim's legs followed him as she ran for
her life down the side of the hot gravel cone.

But the gravel was deep and crumbly, and Nim's
foot twisted—and she rolled and skidded and tumbled
down the mountain. She picked herself up and went on
running, met Fred by the creek where they'd had their
first rest; and they splashed on through and ran some
more. Nim's breath came in jagged chunks; she was so
hot she thought flames might spurt out of her head like
her own miniature volcano.

And just when they couldn't run any farther, they

splashed into the waterfall's cold water and *whoosh*ed gently down to the pool.

They sat in it for one refreshing moment and then ran the rest of the way back to the hut.

Selkie was waiting anxiously on her rock. She barked when she saw them, sniffed Nim all over, and *whuffl*ed sadly when she found the cut on her knee.

It was a big, messy cut, with torn skin, deep gravel grooves, and lots of blood. Nim must have done it when she had tumbled down the mountain but had been too scared to feel it.

It hurt now that she wasn't so scared.

Nim stretched out on the rock and let Selkie fuss. She stared up, and Fire Mountain was still shooting scarlet stars, a glow of red on the gray cone, but the lava hadn't followed them and they were safe at home.

But she hadn't seen Jack's sails, so he wouldn't be home tonight, which meant there was one more thing she had to do. She took her fishing rod back to the rocks, and when she caught a fish, she dropped it in a bucket.

Because sometimes Galileo came when he was called, and sometimes he didn't, but he always came if he saw a fish.

Dear Jack,

Today I climbed Fire Mountain to see if you were coming, but you weren't.

I didn't do any science measurements or write anything down because the volcano erupted when we were at the top. If you think Fred can move fast for coconut, you should see how fast he can run away from an exploding volcano!

I think I can see Galileo now, so I'll say good-bye.

Love (as much as Chica loves soccer),

Nim

A frigate bird came closer, and it was Galileo, so Nim danced the fish in the air and called his name. Galileo swooped low and stayed long enough for her to pull out the letter that was tucked into his band and stick hers in instead.

"Thank you!" Nim called as the big bird soared up to his nest on the cliffs, and she unrolled Jack's letter.

Dear Nim,

Worked out best way of fixing rudder is to drill hole through tip (not easy underwater!), pass a rope through hole, and steer with rope.

Have drilled hole but had to jump out before I could get rope through it. Sharks around here must have tasted the chunk I lost from my forehead in the storm, thought it was jaw-snapping yum!, and wanted to chomp the rest.

Soon as they forget about me, I'll get that rope through

and be on my way home! But the storm blew me a long
way, so it'll take a couple of days.

Love (as much as sails love wind),
Jack

Nim read the letter, and then she read it again. And even though Jack had tried to make it funny, she felt more lonely and miserable than she ever had before. Even writing a long, long e-mail to tell Alex Rover all about Fire Mountain didn't make her feel better.

8

WHILE JACK WAS waiting for the sharks to disappear and hoping that he could fix his rudder and worrying about Nim, he saw a ship.

Jack danced a jig and sang a song because he wanted to get home even more than he didn't want to be rescued. His song didn't rhyme and it didn't have a tune, but it went:

"I'll be home soon!
I'll see Nim tomorrow!
The plankton can wait
And everything will be all right!"

The ship came closer.

It was a cruise ship. A pink-and-purple cruise ship.

It was the Troppo Tourists.

Jack stopped dancing and stopped singing, his face was pale and his stomach was sick, but Nim had been alone too long and he knew what he had to do.

In the cabin, he found the flags he'd never used: one with blue-and-white checks and the other striped. When he put them up together, they said SOS: COME AND RESCUE ME! to any sailor who saw them.

Then he waited. The longer he waited, the more he didn't want the Troppo Tourists to see the island; he didn't want to talk to them and didn't want them oohing and aahing and taking pictures of his home, but the longer he waited, the more he didn't want Nim to be alone.

The sad flags fluttered from the mast, and he went on waiting.

But the Troppo Tourists sailed out of sight.

EARLY NEXT AFTERNOON, when Nim was sitting in a palm tree to watch for Jack, the ship came to the island.

Just a speck in the distance, so Nim cheered and thought how she would run to the farthest point of Keyhole Cove and blow her shell-whistle and shout:

"JACK NEEDS HELP! LOOK FOR A BOAT WITH A BROKEN RUDDER!"

Then she saw the colors through the spyglass, and she knew that she could never ever call out to this ship. Because no matter how much she wanted Jack to be home now, what she wanted even more was for him to be happy, and he'd never be happy if the Troppo Tourists came to the island.

And even though they didn't know it was Jack's island,

if they passed the blue waters of Keyhole Cove or the peaceful sands of Turtle Beach, they'd know it was the most beautiful island in the world. They'd come back with curious tourists and fill up the island with holidays and noise.

"Oh, no they won't!" said Nim.

She raced to the hut and turned on the laptop.

To: aka@incognito.net
From: jack.rusoe@explorer.net
Date: Tuesday 6 April, 14:14
Dear Alex Rover,

I hope it's okay to write so early, but could you please tell me right away what your hero would do if the bad guys were coming to his island and he wanted them to go away and not notice it.
From Nim

To: jack.rusoe@explorer.net
From: aka@incognito.net
Date: Tuesday 6 April, 9:17
Dear Nim,

It's okay to write anytime (and it doesn't even have to be about coconuts!)—unless your parents have another rule.

When my beautiful lady hero was escaping from bad guys in **Sands at Sunset,** she disguised herself in old clothes and grease till she looked so ugly they didn't notice her. But a whole island is trickier!

Somehow the hero would have to make the rocks seem more dangerous, the reef more terrifying, the pale sands bleak and lonely—make the whole island seem like a creepy, scary place.

This sounds like an exciting game!
Your friend, Alex

The ship was coming closer. Nim would have to work fast to disguise the island.

The sea lions were on their rocks, coughing, barking, honking, all the usual sea lion conversation, but Nim interrupted, shouting and waving her arms. Selkie swam after her, barking reproachfully.

The ship came closer still. It was slowing down—it had seen the island. "Bad boat!" Nim screamed.

Selkie looked confused. The other sea lions stared.

"Shoo!" Nim shouted. "Get off the rocks!" Grumbling and grunting, they slid into the water. Nim dived in after them, but Selkie blocked her before she'd gone three strokes.

"I'll go back," Nim pleaded, "if you stop the boat."

So when Nim was safely on the shore, Selkie headed the other sea lions out to the reef.

The ship stopped and lowered a small boat down to the water.

Creeping low, out of sight of snooping binoculars, Nim jumped into the tidal pools and snatched up armfuls of the iguanas' favorite seaweed.

The small boat cast off with a snarl of its motor, and the king of the sea lions bellowed back.

If a boat found its way in through the maze of the reef, Shell Beach would be the first thing it would see.

Crawling across the pebbly rocks and sharp white shells, the blood flowing red from the cut on her knee, Nim threw handfuls of seaweed from one end of the beach to the other. Fred followed, nibbling as fast as she could put it down.

"You can have coconut," she promised him, "if you'll bring all your friends to the beach."

Fred looked at her. "As much coconut as you can eat," Nim said.

With a sneeze of surprise, Fred scuttled away—from rock to rock, tidal pool to sea—until the beach was covered by spiny iguanas munching free seaweed. From the reef it would look like a beach of bumpy gray rocks.

And maybe they would turn around before they saw Turtle Beach.

Nim sneaked back to her Lookout Palm, shimmied to the top, and clung high and still.

The boat had nearly reached the first gap in the reef. It was close enough for Nim to see the people inside, wearing pink T-shirts and purple caps with a stuffed fish on top.

Suddenly the gap disappeared in a swirling, thrashing sea lion storm. The boat idled on past, looking for another place to get through—but the sea lions followed. The king roared his roar and the others bellowed; the splashing sprayed higher and the boat rocked wildly, and was slowly, ferociously, pushed out to sea.

From her tree, Nim could see something else. Galileo was circling the boat.

Galileo had never seen pretend fish before. Galileo's rule was that if it looked like a fish, it *was* a fish, and if someone else had that fish, Galileo would steal it.

He called to his mate, and they dived together to snatch two fish caps from the heads in the boat.

The people screamed and swore, throwing their arms over their faces, but the giant birds only cared about the caps. They spat the first ones into the sea and snatched two more to see if they tasted better.

Now the boat jolted, tipping hard as if it had hit a rock.

"Please don't get hurt!" Nim begged the sea lions.

The boat steadied. Its engine roared and shot it back across the water.

The tide was going out. By the time the little boat had been lifted onto the ship, the reef was jagged above the water.

So the Troppo Tourists cruised on past, but they didn't go away. They went as slow and as close as they dared, past Turtle Beach and round the point of Frigate Bird Cliffs.

Nim crept down to the beach and tried not to cry.

Chica lumbered up from the water, a smug look on her face and purple paint across her shell. Nim remembered the jolt. "Did you hit them?" she asked, scratching under the turtle's chin.

Chica looked smugger. Everyone tried but me, thought Nim. It stinks!

Turtle Beach stank, too—stank worse than a bad day at the Hissing Stones. "Yuck!" said Nim.

Half a dead shark had washed up in the tide.

"No one would land if they could smell that!" said Nim, and wondered if Alex Rover's hero would use a rotten shark to fight for his island.

She sprinted to the hut and grabbed her wagon; dumped in the shark, slimy and rotting. It was a long, puffing haul to the Hissing Stones but Nim would have pulled it to the top of Fire Mountain if she'd had to.

The steam was drifting out to sea. It wasn't an extra-stinky day, but "I'll fix that!" said Nim.

She dragged the shark out of the wagon and across the biggest vent, where steam hissed out between the stones.

The steam stopped coming out, and the shark didn't smell any worse than it had before.

"What else stinks?" Nim wondered. Sometimes seaweed washed up on the Black Rocks. If it didn't dry out and it didn't wash away, after a while it began to rot. Nim scrambled

up and collected shirtfuls of putrid sea muck. She poked her head around the point. The ship was cruising past the breakers where the Black Rocks met the reef.

Nim clutched her seaweed and tumbled down boulders to the Hissing Stones. The shark smelled so bad now that she wanted to vomit, but she dumped the seaweed onto the steaming vents and ran back to hide, out of the stench and out of sight.

The ship rounded the point.

For a long, long moment, nothing happened. Nim had dumped so much muck that no steaming stink could escape.

It was too late to do anything else.

The ship was across from Sea Lion Point, right in line with the Hissing Stones.

The shark exploded.

The rotting seaweed fountained.

The built-up steam sprayed bits of rotten shark, seaweed, and Nim-didn't-know-what in a rushing geyser far into the air. The gentle breeze wafting out to sea turned into a gray, choking, sick-making fog.

The ship turned and steamed out of sight.

THAT EVENING NIM was so tired she couldn't eat. And she felt so cold and empty inside, and so hot and itchy outside, that she took her flashlight and towel and went up to the pool.

Nim loved the ocean because it was always there, wherever she looked and as far as she could see, but it was too huge and powerful to understand and too dangerous to trust. The pool was easy to love because it was so small that she knew every rock in it, and so peaceful she could float peacefully as the sky got darker and the moon and stars came out, while the muck and muddling washed away.

9

TODAY MIGHT BE the day that Jack comes home, Nim thought, and the day to make Alex Rover's raft.

She jumped out of bed.

"Oh, no you don't!" her knee screamed, and she sat down again even faster. Her knee was puffy and hot, red with oozy blood and yellow with pus.

"Yuck!" said Nim, but she got up again.

Very slowly she hobbled down to the rocks with a breakfast coconut. Fred had remembered her promise. "You'll pop!" Nim exclaimed after the fifth piece of coconut, but Fred went on eating.

Washed up on the beach, just below Selkie's rock, were two purple caps with ridiculous fish on top. "*That's* an easier way to call Galileo!" said Nim, and picked them up.

Behind the caps was a big piece of driftwood, and under the driftwood was a torn piece of fishing net.

Nim and Jack hated fishing nets, but—"The raft!" said Nim.

The net was torn too jagged to make one big bag, but she could cut four squares and make two smaller rafts instead.

The net cord was tough and slippery. After a few cuts, Nim had to get her sharpening stone, drawing her pocket-knife across it the way Jack had taught her, one side and then the other, faster and again, till sparks flew and the blade was smooth and fine.

The sun said it was long past lunchtime when she finished cutting. Her knee hurt too much to go up to the vegetable garden, so she ate the last banana with some limpets and seaweed from Shell Beach, and drank the juice from a coconut because there was no water left, either.

Then, sitting in the shade of a palm tree, she knotted the squares down the sides and across the bottom. She flicked the net—knot and pull—and Fred peekabooed from side to side. Selkie grabbed the end of the net in her teeth and tugged.

It's not easy working on something when a sea lion is playing tug-of-war with the other end. It took a long time to finish the two bags, then a long, sore limp to Keyhole Cove.

Selkie and Fred jumped in to help fish out the coconuts, which would have been more helpful if they hadn't kept playing coconut soccer instead.

"Stop being STUPID!" Nim screamed.

Fred sank to the bottom and hid behind a giant clam. Selkie *humph*ed onto the reef with her back to Nim.

Nim, feeling smaller than the limpets she'd eaten for lunch, crawled up beside her. "I'm sorry," she whispered.

Selkie could never stay angry for long, but Fred could. Nim had to dive three times before she could coax him back up.

When she had all the coconuts on the rocks, Nim loaded ten into each bag and tied knots across the top so they couldn't escape. The sun was low over the sea by the time she dumped the second bag back into the cove and climbed on top.

The first three times she tried, the bag raft ended up on top of her instead of the other way around. The fourth time Nim won.

She lay on her stomach and Fred rode on her back; she

paddled once right around the cove, but she was in more of a floating mood today and the raft was good at that, too.

But not with a sea lion on top. Selkie thumped onto the other one and sank straight to the bottom.

"Try both together!" said Nim, trying not to laugh.

Nim held the rafts and Selkie hauled herself on. She floated across the cove, nosing herself off the shore and bumping from reef to rocks. She liked it so much, she forgot to tease Fred; she could have played there all night, but:

"Sun's nearly set!" said Nim. "E-mail time."

To: aka@incognito.net
From: jack.rusoe@explorer.net
Date: Wednesday 7 April, 18:25
Dear Alex Rover,

This morning I found an old fishing net, so I made two rafts because I thought it would be easier than one big one. They are lots of fun to ride; Selkie liked them so much she barked till her throat was sore!

In Keyhole Cove, I could ride sitting up, but it's easier lying down, especially if your hero was out at sea with big waves.

Fred and I rode together, and the raft floated so well we would have been dry if we hadn't got so wet getting on! Fred's not very heavy.

Selkie needed two rafts or she sank to the bottom. She's a bit heavier than Jack, so if your hero is about

70

that big he could float on a raft with twenty coconuts.
If I'd known that, I would have made just one big raft
after all, because Selkie sometimes slipped down the
middle and I had to hold the rafts together for her to
get on again. But I guess your hero wouldn't bounce as
much as Selkie!
From Nim

To: jack.rusoe@explorer.net
From: aka@incognito.net
Date: Wednesday 7 April, 13:29
Dear Nim,

Robinson Crusoe couldn't have done better! I'll stop
worrying about how my hero could swim to the island
if he were tied up in a sack. He can do exactly what
you've done—though he'll find a piece of net just the
right size for one big bag, so he won't have to fall
down the middle like poor Selkie!

Here's the scene: he's gasping on the beach,
realizes that he's lying on a fishing net—and, as he
sits up, is nearly bonked on the head by a falling
coconut. Phew! That was close! he thinks. Then—"Aha!"
and he makes his raft, and paddles bravely out to sea
to defeat the bad guys...

Which reminds me—how did your game work out
yesterday?
Yours, Alex

Alex waited, but Nim didn't answer. She'd turned the
Internet and laptop off and was already asleep.

What kind of dog weighs as much as a man? Alex wondered. Selkie must be huge! And Fred must be a dog, too; I can't imagine a cat riding a raft.

She stared out the window. From the forty-first floor, she could see a long way, but no matter how hard she tried, she couldn't see Keyhole Cove or a hero on a coconut raft.

And for just a moment, Alex wished that she could be a person who *did* things instead of writing them ... who could sail across seas or live happily on a tropical island.

But Alexandra Rover was a dreamer, not a doer. She was stuck in place like a train on a track, as much a part of the city as the post office steps.

IN THE MORNING, Nim's knee was hotter and fatter, with red lines streaking around the ooze.

She didn't want to walk anywhere or do anything, but she had no water to drink and no food to eat, so Fred climbed on her shoulders and she pulled her wagon slowly up to the vegetable garden. She filled her bottles from the waterfall, cut off a bunch of bananas, picked some strawberries, and rode back down the hill.

Selkie huffed anxiously. "I'll feel better after a swim," Nim said.

So they swam around to Turtle Beach. Chica was grazing for seaweed, but she stopped to play a very lazy game of coconut soccer—though it was more like catch, because nobody could be bothered to wrestle for the nut.

The tide was going out, and when they'd finished the game, Nim lay on her stomach and dug for clams with an old shell, while Selkie and Fred galumphed around the wet sand and Chica watched and nodded.

When she'd scooped out enough for dinner, Nim made a fire, baked her clams, and split the coconut for dessert.

Fred darted his nose under her arm and nearly got bopped on the head with her coconut-breaking rock. "Get out of the way, you greedy dragon!" she teased, and broke him off a piece.

Shining there, like a perfect surprise, was a round, creamy pearl.

Nim stared, not wanting to touch or move it. Jack had told her that sometimes, once in a lifetime or so, a coconut could make a pearl just the same way an oyster did, but Nim had never thought she'd see one.

Fred finished his own coconut—snapped—and the pearl disappeared.

And Nim felt as if everything good in her life had disappeared, too, and she knew it wasn't true and she knew it was silly, but she cried till her shirt was soggy and her breath was hiccupy and the tears didn't know how to stop.

Fred sat staring with his mouth full of coconut and pearl.

Selkie *whump*ed him on the back with her flipper—and chunks of coconut and the pearl flew out of his mouth.

Nim gave one last hiccup and took the pearl back to the hut.

It was even more beautiful when it was clean, more wonderful than a shell's gleaming inside whorls, because it was whole and perfect. "A lucky pearl," Nim whispered, because anything so rare must be lucky, and to be beautiful and rare must be the luckiest of all.

She put it on a piece of stroked-smooth driftwood in front of her mother's picture and, since it was nearly sunset now anyway, turned on the laptop.

The light glowed, the computer hummed, but just as she clicked the e-mail box open, the screen went black. She'd forgotten to charge the battery.

The pearl didn't seem so lucky when she couldn't tell Alex Rover about it.

THE NEXT MORNING, the red lines and the yellow ooze, angrier and pussier than the day before, were back on Nim's knee. Her body was warm and her head was as fat and floaty as a cloud.

The solar panel was okay, the laptop battery was charging ... the other charts and chores didn't seem to matter. She didn't feel like breakfast, but Selkie fussed until she had a glass of water and a banana.

Galileo swooped past, chasing a booby bird with a fish in its beak.

Another letter was sticking out of his band.

"Thank you, Troppo Tourists!" said Nim, grabbing the paper as Galileo snatched the fish cap from her hand.

Dear Nim,

Great news! Your fix-it father has got a fixed-up rudder—I'm on my way home!

Plankton celebrated, too—put on a great show last night—AND I discovered a new species of dinoflagellate protozoan zooplankton!

(It doesn't look EXACTLY like you but I named it after you anyway.)

Protozoan
Nim ←

    The wind's against me, but if it doesn't get worse, I'll be home tomorrow night or the day after.
    Love (as much as big plankton love little plankton),
    Jack

Nim knew she ought to be happy and ought to write a letter back, but her knee hurt too much to care and she needed advice faster than Galileo could bring it.

    She dozed beside Selkie and, when she was too hot, went back to the hut. The battery was charged.

    Just for a moment, she wondered if Alex Rover still wanted to write to her now the rafts were finished, but there was no one else to ask.

To: aka@incognito.net
From: jack.rusoe@explorer.net
Date: Friday 9 April, 10:48
Dear Alex Rover,
    I'm sorry I couldn't write yesterday because I

forgot to do the science stuff, so the battery wasn't strong enough to turn on the e-mail.

What would your hero do if he cut his knee when he climbed Fire Mountain and now it has red lines and yellow gunk and his head feels hot and cloudy?

Also, does your hero get lonely and miserable when he's on the island and the lady hero is with the bad guys? And even if he finds a coconut pearl, it doesn't seem as pretty because there's no one to share it with, because Selkie and Fred don't care about things like that (except when Fred tries to eat it, but that doesn't count).

From Nim

ALEX HAD WOKEN long before daylight with the story dancing in her mind like images from a film. She saw swaying palms and hot gold sand, a shimmering waterfall and grumbling volcano, clear blue sea and cloudless sky ...

As the sun came up, she looked out at the dawn gray roofs and railways and put on the CD *Sea Bird Songs and Dolphin Duets*. "Just like being by the sea!" the blurb claimed.

"Not quite," said Alex, turning on the computer.

She read Nim's e-mail and she turned quite pale.

"It can't be true!" said Alex. "A kid can't be all by herself on an island!" And she read it again.

77

Then she printed out all of Nim's other e-mails and read them again, and she looked at the map she'd drawn. She read Nim's e-mail about climbing Fire Mountain and what the island looked like, and realized that Nim never ever mentioned another person.

"If one real thing has happened in my life," said Alex, "this is it."

To: jack.rusoe@explorer.net
From: aka@incognito.net
Date: Friday 9 April, 5:55
Dear Nim,

If my hero's knee were very swollen and sore, he would soak it in the sea and then clean it up with fresh coconut juice and bandage it. Then he'd REST in the shade and drink LOTS of water.

And if he felt lonely and miserable he'd tell someone—maybe on an e-mail.

That's what girl heroes on real islands should do, too.

Are you alone? Where are your parents?

Do you need help?

Love, Alex

Nim read the letter fast and turned off the computer. Her knee still hurt, but it didn't seem as bad now she knew what to do. She took her blue water bottle down to the beach and sat in the shade of a rock with her legs in the

78

water. Selkie sat on one side and worried, and Fred sat on the other side and slept, and Nim sipped her water and dreamed in the middle.

When she woke up, she was stiff and sore, and the sun was going down. "I've been here all day!" said Nim, and she didn't know if Alex Rover's hero would have sat there that long, but she liked the way her head felt as if it belonged to her again. Then she took a clean hanky from the hut, punched a hole in a coconut, and wiped the yellow pus and slimy muck away from her knee, and now the knee was sore but not hot and fat. And she turned on the laptop and read Alex Rover's letter again.

"Oh!" said Nim, and felt pink and happy, because if Alex Rover wanted to come and rescue her, then he really must be a hero, just like the newspaper story said.

Even if she didn't need to be rescued.

To: aka@incognito.net
From: jack.rusoe@explorer.net
Date: Friday 9 April, 18:26
Dear Alex Rover,

My mother went to investigate the contents of a blue whale's stomach when I was a baby, but some bad guys frightened the whale and she hasn't been seen since.

Jack is studying plankton. He went away for three days, except his rudder got broken in a storm and so did his satellite dish, but he sent me a message with Galileo the frigate bird to say he'll be home soon.

Soon might be tomorrow or the day after that.

I'm not alone because Fred and Selkie are here, and so is Chica.

So I don't really need help because I washed my knee like you said and it feels a lot better. And I'm happy that you're really your hero, because I always knew you were.

From Nim

But when she turned off the laptop, she didn't feel quite so bright and brave, so instead of going to bed, she called Fred and Selkie and they went down to Turtle Beach and sat with Chica till the full moon shone silver on the waves.

Chica would leave soon to wander the world's oceans for another year. "But you'll come back next spring, won't you?" said Nim, because it was hard to think of Chica leaving, too, when Jack wasn't home yet and Alex didn't need to rescue her.

Chica nodded sleepily.

"And maybe then," Nim said, "Alex will come and meet you, too."

11

"It's a nightmare," Alex groaned, keying in *Travel Agents* in the Internet search engine. "She's alone on the island and nobody knows about it except me. *Me!*—who's been afraid of airplanes and oceans since my uncle whirled me through the air and into a swimming pool!

"I like being in my flat," she moaned, clicking Pacific Charter Flights, "with my books, my computer, and my imaginary friends. People who live in my head and go away when I put their story away. Places that fit into maps and pictures. Animals that don't smell or eat or leave hair on the carpet.

"There's only one thing to do," she said, clicking back to her e-mail.

To: jack.rusoe@explorer.net
From: aka@incognito.net
Date: Friday 9 April, 13:52
Dear Nim,

All my heroes are just pretend. Real people aren't usually as brave—or as strong or smart or lucky—as the heroes in my stories. Maybe that's why it's fun to make them up or read about them.

Because I'm not tall, dark, and handsome; I'm certainly not brave—and I'm not a man.

But even if I'm not a hero, and you don't need rescuing, I'd still love to come and see you, and the island—and, of course, Fred, Selkie, and Chica. (What kind of dog is Selkie? I'm guessing that she's a Saint Bernard, if she weighs more than your father. And Fred's little—a poodle?)

Love, Alex

P.S. My phone number is 155 897 346. What's yours?

The letter waited, all the next day, till Nim checked her e-mail again.

She stared at the screen. She read the letter out loud and the words stayed the same.

She turned the computer off and ripped out the plug, but the words danced in her head.

Alex Rover was not a hero. Alex Rover was a woman, and she wasn't even brave.

Outside, the evening was peaceful and still, but inside,

Nim was a rage hotter than Fire Mountain's lava and wilder than a whirlpool in a storm.

She felt angry and cheated, tricked and stupid, lost and lonely, sad and confused—and the feelings were stronger than the words could say. They jostled and shoved, spun, crowded, and exploded.

Her shout rang across the water; birds settling for the night flapped into the sky, and the king roared an answer from Sea Lion Point.

Selkie, barking worriedly, lolloped across the sand. Fred peered from under his rock.

Nim was afraid that if she used the laptop she'd punch the keys right through the keyboard. She grabbed a piece of paper and a pencil and marched back outside.

To Alex Rover,

It was horrible to trick me even if you didn't mean to, because whenever I was really lonely or scared or bored, I thought about what you would do and then I could do it, too. Which was stupid if you're not a hero, and I wish I'd never done it and I especially wish that I'd never ever wished that you were my father instead of Jack.

I will never forgive you.

Good-bye forever from Nim

Scrabbling in the dark, she found sticks and branches for a fire and, when it was blazing, threw her letter on top so that the smoke would carry it far, far away to wherever Alex Rover lived, and she would smell it and know just how angry Nim was.

Selkie and Fred crept up beside her. "Alex Rover lied to me!" Nim told them, and threw another stick on the fire.

Selkie barked low in her chest.

"Well, not exactly *lied*," Nim muttered, and rubbed tears on Selkie's warm fur, "but she's not a hero. I thought I knew who Alex Rover was . . . he was my friend and now he's gone!"

Selkie grunted comfortingly.

"You won't change into something else, will you?" Nim asked, not sure whether she was joking or not. "I won't wake up tomorrow and find out you're a mermaid?"

Selkie grunted again, a little louder.

"Alex thinks you're a Saint Bernard . . . and she thinks Fred is a *poodle*! She must be crazy!"

Suddenly she began to giggle.

"She thought you were dogs and I thought she was a hero!"

The giggle became a laugh, the laugh became a bellow, and she was rolling over and over on the sand, hiccuping and laughing, or crying, she didn't know which, until Fred

sneezed and Selkie barked to make her stop whichever
it was.

And she knew there was another reason that she'd sent
the letter in a way that Alex couldn't read it.

So when the sun came up next morning, she turned
on the laptop again.

To: aka@incognito.net
From: jack.rusoe@explorer.net
Date: Sunday 11 April, 6:45
Dear Alex Rover,
    Maybe you didn't try to trick me. I wanted to know
someone brave because I'm not.
    I think maybe I accidentally tricked you, too. Selkie
and Fred aren't dogs, but you will like them.
    When are you coming?
From Nim

To: jack.rusoe@explorer.net
From: aka@incognito.net
Date: Sunday 11 April, 1:46
Dear Nim,
    Now.
Love, Alex

For two nights and two days, Alex had been planning,
sorting, packing.

Her time had switched to island time; she slept when

it was night there and got up in the dark to turn on her computer at the island's dawn.

She'd refused to think about what she'd do if Nim said no. Because she didn't quite believe that Nim had stopped being lonely, and she didn't quite know if Jack would really be home soon.

And because nothing in her life had ever been this important.

She packed a first-aid kit, her laptop and cell phone, two notebooks and two pens, *The Swiss Family Robinson* and *Robinson Crusoe*, a toothbrush, a hairbrush, soap, two T-shirts, two pairs of shorts, one pair of jeans, one sweater, three sets of underwear and socks, and the map with the island marked with a dot. Then she picked up her suitcase and locked the door behind her.

12

THE FIRST PLANE was a jet, big and solid, with nearly four hundred passengers and more crew than Alex could count.

"Alex Rover!" exclaimed the flight attendant. "The world-famous adventure writer?"

"I guess so," said Alex.

"Come and meet the pilot—he'll be so excited!"

"You," Alex told herself, "are a weak-kneed, spineless jellyfish."

"Pardon?"

"I'd love to," said Alex, and followed her into the cockpit.

"Alex Rover!" said the pilot, blushing red as a stoplight. "I always wondered—I mean . . . Would you like to fly the plane?"

"No thanks!"

"Not exciting enough for you?" And he showed her interesting things about the jet's instrument panel and engines.

All Alex could think about was what a very long way down the ground was; then the ground turned to ocean, and that didn't make her feel happier at all.

They landed after the sun had set, and when Alex found the little plane that would take her to the island nearest to Nim's, the pilot said they couldn't leave until morning.

"I can't land on that island in the dark," he said. "I'm not a daredevil like you!"

I'm not a daredevil, Alex wanted to say. I just need to get to Nim's island right away.

In the hotel room, the feeling was stronger. She felt like a tiger in a cage, trying to burst free.

Instead, she checked her e-mail.

To: aka@incognito.net
From: jack.rusoe@explorer.net
Date: Sunday 11 April, 18:28
Dear Alex,

I can't believe you're really coming! How will you get here and how long will it take?

I forgot to give you my phone number before. It's 022 446 579.

I've never talked to anyone before except Jack but I guess it works the same way.
From Nim

To: jack.rusoe@explorer.net
From: aka@incognito.net
Date: Sunday 11 April, 22:00
Dear Nim,

Curses, curses! I can't go any farther tonight, and now it's too late to phone!

I'm flying to Sunshine Island at dawn, to meet a boat from the adventure-cruise company Troppo Tourists. They've been as friendly as a salesman with a sick car to sell—and have offered to take me right to your island, though I haven't told them yet where it is.

Nim, it's been so much fun writing to you—no matter what happens, I'm glad I tried to come and meet you.

See you tomorrow!

Love, Alex

NIM WOKE UP when it was still dark, excited as Christmas. She switched on the lamp and checked the e-mail.

ALEX HIT THE alarm clock, and it went on ringing. She reached for her phone.

"They're the bad guys!" a girl's voice shouted.

"Who?" said Alex. "What?"

And then she realized. "The Troppo Tourists?"

"*They* chased the whale when my mother died. Now they want to bring people to stare at us and bother the animals—and Jack hates them. You can't bring them here!"

"No," said Alex. "I think we need to fix them once and for all."

"How?"

"I've got four hours—I'll think of something."

The strangest thing, Nim thought when she hung up, was that it hadn't felt strange talking to Alex.

By the time the sun was properly up, Alex had showered, dressed, and eaten a hotel breakfast and was waiting at the airport, but she still hadn't thought of how to get to Nim's island and keep it secret from the Troppo Tourists.

"Any daredevil plans?" the pilot joked as he started the engine. "Going to parachute out halfway for your next book?"

"That's not a bad idea," Alex muttered. "I couldn't be more scared jumping out of a plane than staying in."

The pilot went as pale as Alex's knuckles. "But there's no land between here and where we're going!"

Alex studied the map and decided he was right: Nim's island was too far away for a detour in this little plane. Besides, she still had to meet the Troppo Tourists— the real bad guys, the reason that Nim didn't have a mother. If Alex didn't turn up, they might go on looking for Nim's island.

This time they might find it.

Alex's fear disappeared, as suddenly and completely as if it had fallen out of the plane without a parachute.

Instead she was angry. For the first time, she knew

exactly how her hero felt when he was fighting the bad guys: "And," she muttered, "I'm going to win!"

The pilot was still worried that she was going to jump out the window. "We're nearly there," he said. "The airport's just past the sailing school—you can see the little boats now."

Alex stared out and tried not to notice that her stomach was diving faster than the plane. That's interesting, she thought. I can feel angry and sick at the same time!

"Do they give lessons?" she asked, because if she was talking she mightn't throw up.

"Give lessons, sell boats . . . Is your next book about sailing?"

"Partly," said Alex. She couldn't talk very well because a sneaky little fear had crept back and she was holding her breath to help the plane land.

Two hours later, she was wetter than she'd ever been and knew more than she'd ever wanted to about the way small sailboats flip upside down and how it feels to be the person flipping off them. But she also knew how to get back on and push the boat right side up, and how to pull the sails and steer.

And she was the owner of a small blue sailboat.

"Not bad for a beginner," the sailing-school owner said, pocketing her money. "But don't go too far from the shore!"

Alex tried to smile.

"Funny," the woman continued, "you've got the same name as the adventure writer. But I don't reckon he'd need sailing lessons!"

"Neither do I, now!" Alex told herself. "I'm ready to go!" And she tried to believe it.

She loaded her suitcase into the little boat and sailed out of the sailing-school cove, around the corner to the pink-and-purple Troppo Tourists ship.

"Ahoy there!" she shouted, jumping onto the wharf and standing up as tall and brave as she could.

The captain came running down the gangplank. "*You're* Alex Rover? But you're ... what a delightful surprise!"

"Are you going to write a book about us?" asked one of the crew.

"Maybe," said Alex.

"We'll have to make a good impression," the captain said, smiling and trying to suck his stomach in behind his Troppo T-shirt.

"I'm sure you will," said Alex. "Do you mind if I bring my little boat?"

"You there!" the captain shouted at two of the crew. "Hoist this boat up on deck."

"Now," he went on, rubbing his hands excitedly, "can you tell us where this island is?"

Alex pointed to a spot on the chart, a little way east of Nim's island.

"We'd love to hear more about it," the captain said, and started the motor.

The crew gathered round as Alex began.

Alex was a storyteller. She spent her life telling stories on paper, and she made people laugh and cry and hold their breath, but she had never told a story as important as this.

She spoke quietly, and the crew huddled nearer, caught in the net of her words.

"Long, long ago, when the world was young, a volcano began to grow, deep under the sea. It grew slowly, day by day and year by year, pulling lava from the heart of the earth—rolling, boiling, melting rock, hotter than fire, hot as the sun.

"Then, one bright summer day—a day just like today, a day just like a million other bright summer days—the mountain under the sea *exploded*."

She hissed the word out, her hands and eyes opening wide. The crew shivered.

"With a roar that shook the earth, a storm came: lightning flashed and thunder crashed; winds howled and waves towered. From the heart of the volcano, melted rock and boiling lava poured up and out, higher and higher. And when it had finished and the boiling rock had cooled to stone, the tiny underwater mountain had become a full-grown island with its head poking out from the sea.

"Now, some islands," Alex went on as the Troppo Tourists sat silent and still around her, "become peaceful once they've been born from the sea. But this island didn't. This island stayed hot and angry.

"Its volcano still shoots fire; boiling lava still tumbles down its slopes and the stench of hell floats in its mists. Its rocks are black and sharp and its cliffs are steep."

"No golden sand?" the captain asked hopefully.

"A little," Alex admitted. "But in front of the sands, curved from the rocks at one end to the cliffs at the other, is a maze of rocky reef—a treacherous, sword-sharp, boat-ripping reef."

The crew shivered.

"Lions of the sea," Alex continued, "live on the rocks: the smartest sea lions you will ever meet, the fiercest and bravest in all the world, ready to fight to protect their home.

"And if a boat could pass the sea lions, and find its way through the sword-sharp maze, and not choke in the rotten-egg gas or fry in the boiling lava, when it reached the beach it would meet the dragons."

"Dragons?" squeaked a crew member.

"Small dragons—but so many they could cover the sand, and, like the sea lions, they will fight bravely to save their island."

She hurried on before anyone could ask how.

"There are birds, too, birds who are big and strong and tough enough to live on a mountain that shoots fire and choking gas. Birds who are so quick and agile that they can swoop down and snatch the hairs right out of a person's head."

The captain twitched his hat nervously around his ears. "Why do you want to go to such a terrible place?"

"It sounds even worse than that island last week," one of the crew said. "I'm not going there!"

"You don't need to," Alex said. "You're going to lower my little boat and I'll sail the rest of the way."

"But why?" the captain repeated.

"To see if that's how my hero escapes from the bad guys," Alex lied, because she knew that if they saw the island, they might forget her story.

The captain giggled. "That makes us sound like the bad guys!"

"It depends," said Alex, and began the second part of her story, because it wasn't enough to make them frightened, and now she wanted to make them feel so bad that they would *never ever* bother Nim and Jack again.

"My hero is a sad, lonely man who once lived happily with a lady hero and their baby, helping the world with research and science. But one day, while the lady hero was deep under the sea studying a whale, a noisy boat came to spy on them. My hero *begged* that noisy boat to go away, to be quiet, to stay away from the frightened

97

whale—but they laughed, were louder, and chased that whale so that it swam right to the bottom of the sea—and the lady hero was never seen again."

She whispered the last words. One of the crew sniffed, and one blew his nose, and the others wiped their eyes.

"Are they bad guys?" Alex asked. "You'll have to decide. Because that's not the end of the story."

"Now my heroes live on this fiery, dangerous island, far away from good people and bad. But what if the noisy boat came back, with people to trample their lonely home; to fight their sea lion and dragon friends, and destroy the science they're giving the world?"

Tears dripped onto Troppo shirts; there were gulps and sobs and soggy noses. "That would be a terrible ending!" said the crew. "You can't end a story like that!" And they sobbed some more.

Alex looked at the captain.

The captain didn't care about Nim and Jack; but he was afraid of sea lions and dragons and boat-ripping reefs. And he was *very, very* afraid of being in Alex's book, because people wouldn't pay lots of money to go on Troppo Tourists tours if they knew the captain was a bad guy.

His eyes were sharp and cold as a shark's, but he tried to smile. "A story should have a happy ending," he said. "Your heroes can stay alone on their island, and the tourists can find somewhere else to explore."

13

NIM SANG AS she did her chores. She didn't know how Alex would beat the bad guys, but she knew she would.

She did her charts and cleaned the hut; dusted, shook, and swept; got new palm fronds to make Alex's bed; arranged sea shells around the coconut pearl and her mother's picture.

She weeded and watered the vegetable garden; ate two bananas and some peas for lunch; and dug up three sweet potatoes and picked a lettuce, an avocado, a tomato, and three handfuls of strawberries for later.

Then she flopped into the pool for a rest and a bath, and she and Fred watched the birds overhead.

They were flying inland, as if it were night.

Something was wrong.

Back at the beach, the sea lions were honking and restless, and Fred's friends were zipping over the rocks, even the oldest scuttling like hatchlings.

Selkie was by the hut, barking anxiously for Nim.

Two more gulls flew past, and then a frigate bird.

"Galileo!" Nim called, running to the hut for a Troppo Tourists cap. "Have you got something for me?"

The big bird swooped, grabbed the stuffed fish, and let Nim pull a note from his band.

Dear Nim,

The birds say there's a storm coming.
GO TO THE EMERGENCY CAVE.

Take the phone, laptop, solar panel, battery charger, and other scientific equipment, and whatever else you have time for—but you *are the only thing that matters. As soon as you see that storm coming, drop everything and get to safety.*

If I can beat the storm, I'll be home tonight or early tomorrow.

Love (as much as a Jack loves a Nim),
Jack

Nim stared up at the sky. It was clear and blue, but the air was so still and heavy on her skin that she knew the birds were telling the truth, and she knew she had to do what Jack said. Nim didn't like the Emergency Cave, but it was better than storms.

And it was much better than being on a boat in a storm, and *much, much* better than being on a boat in a storm when you don't know the storm is coming.

"I've got to warn Alex!" said Nim, and dialed the number.

Alex answered on the second ring. "I've learned to sail and I'm on my way! I've just cast off from the Troppo Tourists ship."

"Get back on it," Nim begged.

But a roar of engines drowned Alex's answer, and when the noise faded into the distance, Alex was saying, "I can see a dot where your island is. I should get there quickly—the captain told me there'd be some wind soon."

"It's not a wind," Nim shouted. "It's a storm!"

And then the satellite dish on the Troppo Tourists ship was too far away, and Alex's phone went dead.

Nim dropped her phone into the wagon. She tucked the coconut pearl into her pocket and pulled down the satellite dish and solar panel. She loaded the picture of her mother and the flashlight, battery charger, laptop, and satellite dish into her wagon, and tied the solar panel on top.

Fred climbed on top of *that* and nearly tipped it all over.

"Walking's good for you!" Nim told him, lifting him down before he tipped it back the other way.

"Meet us at the Emergency Cave!" she called to Selkie. Chica would be safer on the sandy sea bottom off Turtle Beach, but sea lions can't stay underwater forever. Besides, if she couldn't have Jack, Nim wanted Selkie in a storm.

At the Hissing Stones, she had to leave the wagon and carry everything over the black boulders to the cave. The laptop was heavy and she was afraid of dropping it; the solar panel dragged and caught its corners in cracks in the rocks; but in four trips, the whole load was safe in the cave.

"Now stay there!" she ordered Fred. Selkie had stopped to fish, but Nim blew the shell-whistle twice to tell her where they were.

The sea was still flat and calm; there wasn't a breath of wind. "I bet I'm moving all this stuff for nothing!" Nim said crossly as she tugged the wagon back to the hut for the books and Jack's files of notes. They were heavy, and it took six trips to get them from the Stones to the Cave.

One more load! she thought.

This time she grabbed her sleeping mat, water bottles, toothbrush, comb, clothes, and barometer, throwing them into the wagon any old way because now she could see in the distance a whirl of dark air, black and yellow as a bruise, moving across the eastern sky.

It was coming fast—faster than Fred after coconut. Nim dropped the wagon handle and flew across the grassland. The wind hit just as she reached the Black Rocks.

It knocked her backward and whipped her hair; it tore at her eyes and ripped the breath out of her lungs. Selkie grunted encouragement, Fred skittered, and Nim scrambled the rest of the way on her hands and knees. As she reached the mouth of the cave, the first lightning flashed, the first thunder boomed, and the rain came down like a surf wave on the rocks.

ALEX PULLED HER sails tight, the way the instructor had shown her. The Troppo Tourists ship disappeared; she was alone on a wide, empty ocean in a boat as small and frail as a bathtub toy...

I wish Nim was right and I was my hero! she thought. But at least I can take notes about sailing—the gentle breeze, the interesting clouds...

The interesting clouds came closer, fast. They were

dark gray and swirling. The gentle breeze jumped to a full-force gale, and Alex felt like the hero in a legend who let the winds escape from the bag they were trapped in.

That was when she remembered that she'd left her life jacket on the ship.

"I'll tie myself to the mast," she said, but before she could reach it, the rain started.

Like being in a car wash! Alex thought. Without a car!

The mast suddenly seemed a long way away, but just beside her was a metal ring with a rope through it. Alex yanked the rope free and tied one end to the ring and the other around her waist.

Then there was nothing to do except try to steer and wonder whether the rope she'd pulled off was important, and if it mattered anyway when the boat was balancing on skyscraper-high waves?

Maybe they weren't quite as tall as skyscrapers. Maybe they weren't much higher than a cottage. Tall enough! thought Alex as she roller-coasted from one to the next.

A fork of lightning exploded into a wave; a crash of thunder hit her ears like a boxer's punch.

Alex threw herself onto her stomach and clung to the tiller. Then the next wave was under her and the wind was howling and hurtling her toward the smudge of Nim's island—"Faster than a city train!" Alex guessed.

She couldn't decide whether that was a good thing or not, but she was beginning to understand how her hero felt when she sent him adventuring: terrified-thrilled; sure he was going to die and so alive that he never wanted to stop.

CRACK!

Her sails billowed like a balloon; the mast lifted and toppled off the boat. There was a sad flap of white and her mast and sails sank out of sight.

"So now it's a rowboat," Alex decided.

She pretended that she was her hero, because he wouldn't mind that his computer and suitcase had washed overboard and were at the bottom of the ocean.

He wouldn't even be scared when he saw that the mast had taken a chunk out of the bottom of the boat as a going-away present, and the sea was coming in to take its place. A hero would simply take off his hat and bail, so that's what Alex did.

The problem was that even when she was being a hero, the waves were still monstrous, the rain was still pouring, and the wind was still roaring, and each time they slammed across a wave, more of the wave came into the boat and, no matter how fast she bailed, less of it went out. The hole was getting bigger, and the bigger it got, the faster the water poured in, and the faster the water poured in, the bigger the hole got.

And the bigger the hole got, the faster the boat sank, as if it were tired of being a boat and wanted to try being a submarine.

And Alex was still tied firmly to it.

"If only I'd been a Brownie," she muttered, frantically trying to untie the pulled-tight rope, "and learned to tie reef knots, or whatever kind of knot it is that you can untie when you need to!"

She tried to undo the knot around her waist first, but when she'd pulled it so tight that she could hardly breathe, she gave up and worked on the other end. She tried with fingers and tried with teeth, spluttering and choking, because now the knot was quite a long way underwater.

Which is where I'm going to be, too, Alex thought, and even though she didn't much like being in the top bit of the ocean, she thought she'd like the bottom even less.

14

NIM LAY ON the floor of the cave with Fred under one arm and Selkie sheltering her back. Through the opening, they could see the rain trickle to a stop and the gale gentle to a wind.

They crept out to look, peering out over the Black Rocks.

The sea was still monstrous. The wind had whipped it to a fury, and it wasn't ready to calm down just because the storm had passed. Towering waves crashed onto the shore; spray foamed white and rainbows fountained into the clearing sky.

It could have been beautiful, if Nim hadn't known that Jack was on the west side of the island, being tossed even farther from home, and Alex was on the east being thrown toward it.

"She'll be smashed on the rocks!" Nim cried.

She searched the horizon with her spyglass. There was no sign of a sail, but there was a speck that could be a boat with someone inside it.

Nim was still scared, but there wasn't enough time to think. She crawled back into the cave and tore a sheet from her notebook.

Dear Jack,
    I've gone to rescue Alex Rover.
    Love, Nim

Selkie was waiting; Fred was starting to slide down to the sea.

"Wait!" Nim shouted. "You can't swim out there by yourself!"

But Fred wasn't by himself. Chica had heard Nim's whistle, a storm-while ago, and had been resting on the seabed as close as she could get to her friends in the cave. Fred scrambled onto her back and hooked his claws to the edge of her shell, staring out over her head.

Nim hugged hard around Selkie's neck and they slid into the water.

It was hard swimming, even for a brave and determined lion of the sea. The waves slammed against them, so hard and so high that sometimes they threw Selkie backward and under the water—which is where sea lions like to swim, but not when they're carrying girls on their backs.

Nim's hair whipped like long, wet ropes, and she gulped salt water with every breath, but she clung as tight as she ever could.

The seventh wave came; a swamping, dumping wave, stronger than Selkie, forcing her down deep below the water; stronger than Nim, ripping her arms away from Selkie's neck and pushing her deeper still, so there was nothing but swirling blue and she didn't know which way was up to the air and which was down to the bottom.

She was whirling ... struggling ... sinking ... but Selkie somersaulted backward and pushed her up through the water till she was spluttering ... coughing ... breathing again.

Then the waves weren't quite so wild; they could ride up them and slide down without going deep under the water. When they were in the valleys, they couldn't see anything but blue, but when they were on the top, they could look around. They saw Chica and Fred, but never Alex.

They went on looking. Looking and looking. On and on.

Now Selkie was too tired to leap across the waves and pretend it was fun, but when Nim tried to be helpful and swim, Selkie honked a cross "NO!," so Nim stayed on. She didn't know if she could have swum in those waves anyway.

She started to worry about what she was going to do if she didn't find Alex.

She started to worry about how big the waves were where Jack was, and how far away they were taking him.

She started to worry about Chica and Fred.

She started to worry about how she'd know when it was time to turn back—and that was the hardest thought of all, because it was the only one she could do something about.

She was worrying so hard that she nearly fell off when Selkie barked again.

Then Selkie didn't seem tired and Nim didn't feel worried; she blew her whistle as hard as she could and they charged across the waves to the small sinking boat.

THE WATER WAS up to Alex's waist, then her chest, and up to her neck; she was spluttering and ducking, and still struggling with the knots under the water.

She tried to think what a hero would do now, but all she could think was that a hero would have known how to untie the knot, and that was no help to her at all. She took a deep breath and wondered if it was the last air she'd taste.

A whistle shrilled—and there was the strangest, most wonderful thing she'd ever seen: a wild-haired girl blowing a shell and riding a sea lion across the waves.

"Ni—" Alex shouted, and then her mouth was underwater, too.

Nim remembered the scene in *Mountain Madness* where the hero was snagged by the rope around his waist as he climbed down a cliff. She grabbed her knife from its

pouch and, as Selkie ducked under the water, Nim cut the rope.

Alex bobbed straight up to the surface.

"Nim Rusoe, I presume?"

The boat gurgled rudely and sank.

They looked at each other and started to giggle, choking with laughter and seawater, and Selkie had to bark twice to remind them that treading water with one arm and holding on to a sea lion with the other, in the middle of a stormy ocean, is not the time to giggle. But when Alex heard Selkie bark, she said, "So you're not a Saint Bernard! But you are a savior!" and they laughed a bit more.

And then they turned back toward the island.

It should have been easier now they were going the same way as the waves, except that the waves were

smashing onto the Black Rocks and they didn't want to do that, so they decided to curve around the reef and come in on the gentle slopes of Shell Beach. And Selkie couldn't carry them both.

"We could take turns swimming and riding," said Nim.

But even going with the waves, Nim couldn't swim as fast as Selkie, so Selkie kept having to turn around, and Alex wasn't very good at riding, so she fell off every time Selkie turned around.

"I wish I'd gone to swimming lessons instead of writing stories about fish!" Alex muttered, and Nim started worrying again. She was getting tired, too, and so the next time Selkie circled back and Alex fell off, they both hung on to Selkie with one arm and swam with the other—but the island didn't seem to be getting much closer.

Suddenly there was a tickle under Nim's arm, and a sweet, spiny head with a grinning dragon face.

"Fred!" she cried—and Alex, who had never seen anything quite as ugly and wonderful as a marine iguana, said, "I'm sorry I called you a poodle."

Following Fred was something that looked like a big bag with something else behind it—and *that* something began to look like a smug green turtle.

Chica had found one of the coconut rafts.

She moved steadily toward them, pushing the raft, disappearing as each wave rolled over her and popping up when it cleared.

Nothing ever upset Chica.

Selkie kept pushing Alex and Nim toward the island; Chica kept coming closer... and finally they met. Alex slid across from Selkie and climbed onto the coconut raft. She lay down and kicked her legs, but kicking Chica in the head didn't seem a good way to thank her, so she crouched forward and paddled with her hands. It didn't make the raft go much faster, but Alex felt better doing something.

Nim got back onto Selkie and Fred climbed onto her shoulders.

A few minutes later they tumbled onto Shell Beach, below where the hut used to be.

15

THE HUT WAS gone, and Nim was too tired to start looking for what was left of it.

The last of the storm clouds disappeared from the sky; the sun sank gold and low, and Nim and Alex were still lying on the beach talking.

Selkie slipped back into the water to fish for her supper. Fred found some seaweed left on the beach by angry waves.

Chica gave them a long look and dragged herself toward the water.

Nim hugged her, as tight as you can hug a large green turtle. "Good-bye till next year!"

"Thank you for rescuing me," Alex said, and kissed the top of Chica's wrinkled head. Chica looked up at her and blinked.

It was always hard to tell what Chica was thinking.

"We need to go to the Emergency Cave before the sun goes down," Nim said. She had a feeling Alex mightn't be very good at rock climbing in the dark. "We can have an emergency can for dinner."

"And a coconut from the raft!"

"I wonder where the other raft went," said Nim, but she was wondering even more where Jack was.

THE OTHER RAFT had been tossed out of Keyhole Cove when the sea went crazy, but it had bounced clear of the swirling reef waters and been caught by the monster waves raging out to the west.

And grabbed by an exhausted man with a scar on his forehead and a two-week-old beard.

ALEX WASN'T ANY better at rock climbing than Nim had thought she'd be, but she loved the cave. "Like Ali Baba's!" she exclaimed.

"I cleaned the hut so nicely!" Nim said gloomily. "I even made you a new sleeping mat!"

Alex hugged her, and it wasn't quite the same as hugging Jack and not quite the same as snuggling into Selkie, but it made her believe that the world might get better again.

NIM WOKE TO see Alex sitting at the door of the cave, watching the sun rise over Fire Mountain. "And look at the sea!" said Alex.

The waves rolled gently, washed clean and blue. Birds

soared and swooped, screeched and fished; iguanas and lizards scrabbled; sea lions lazed and their king's *honk!* echoed across the water.

Selkie *whuff*led good morning. But when Nim had hugged her and rubbed noses, Selkie slid down the rocks, and a moment later her brown head popped up at Sea Lion Point, beside the king's.

Fred grazed for seaweed in the tidal pools. He didn't quite trust this ocean yet.

Nim and Alex had a coconut and emergency rice pudding for breakfast, set up the satellite dish and the solar panel on a flat rock above the cave, plugged the computer and phone in to charge, and went out to explore.

They went to Turtle Beach, Sea Lion Point, the Hissing Stones, and Keyhole Cove—"Where it all began!" said Alex.

"Because if I hadn't done the experiment . . ."

". . . I wouldn't have been able to write back again . . ."

". . . and you would never have come!"

Already that seemed impossible.

They went on exploring. Nim's beautiful island was shredded and messy with bits of hut, pieces of shirts and desk, coconuts, palm branches, broken trees, and lying-down bushes.

"As if a giant had a tantrum!" Alex exclaimed.

The garden was worse. It looked as if Selkie had taken her sea lion family up for a party. Pea plants were mashed, avocados were mushed, and tomatoes were soup. Some plants had so few leaves it was hard to remember what they used to be.

The garden shed, with the bananas still on their hook, had been lifted right over the wall and dropped neatly in the middle of the bamboo grove.

Nim and Alex collected three green pineapples, a few mashed strawberries, and scattered pea pods. They hauled broken bits out of the pool and into the compost heap, and saved two avocados, a tomato, and ten more strawberries.

"And the sweet potatoes will be safe," Nim said, "when we feel like digging them."

They chucked broken plants off the garden and propped up the living ones, and when they were worn out, Nim taught Alex how to slide down the waterfall into the pool, and then Alex told her stories till they were ready to work again.

She told her more stories that night while they tried to sleep on the hard cave floor.

The stories were funny and made Nim laugh; exciting, so she had to hold her breath; and something else that made her feel soft and warm and happy-sad, so she wanted to hug Selkie, except that Selkie had decided it was too hard to go all the way up to the cave for the night and was sleeping with the sea lions.

The next day they started clearing the grasslands and beaches, dragging branches into piles for bonfires and coconuts into heaps for eating, and sorting out anything else that might have come from the hut or could be useful to build a new one.

And all the time that they heaved and carried and sorted, Nim worried about when Jack would get home and when Alex would leave. She hated the stories Alex told about her home in the city, because she wanted to pretend that Alex could stay on the island for ever and ever.

They took a different path to the garden and found Nim's favorite blue glass bottle, her comb, a good piece of rope under a dead jellyfish, and her wagon, hooked on a branch at the top of a tree.

The tree wasn't hard to climb, but it was a long stretch from the last safe branch, and when the wagon tumbled to the ground, so did Nim.

The scab rubbed off her knee, and it began to bleed again. Nim didn't cry, but Alex did.

"I had bandages, cream ... a whole first-aid box for you!" she sobbed.

But she helped Nim clean the sand out with fresh coconut juice, and then Fred hinted that they ought to eat the coconut now they'd opened it, so they had it for lunch with bananas. And since they were at the pool and had a comb, they washed their hair and combed out two days of tangles, which hurt more than the skinned knee.

Alex looked so pretty, tugging the knots out of her long gold hair, and she was still so sad about Nim's knee. "Wait here!" Nim ordered, and ran all the way to the cave and back again without even stopping to look out to sea.

"Close your eyes!" she said, and dropped the coconut pearl into Alex's hands. "I was going to give it to you if you went away, but it seems like you need it now."

"Oh, Nim!" said Alex. "I can't take this!"

"I had it in front of my mother's picture," Nim said. "But a picture can't really see, so I want you to have it."

Alex got soggy again.

"If I could have a daughter," she said when she could talk, "I'd want her to be exactly like you."

Suddenly the honking from the sea lions was too loud to hear anything else. Nim flew down the hill as Selkie led the whole herd into the water, splashing and barking at the strange shape drifting in through the reef.

And Jack staggered off the bag of coconuts and waded onto the sand.

Then he and Nim did a wild "What happened? You're okay?" laughing, hugging dance, but Jack went pale as he stared at where the hut used to be.

"The science stuff is safe," Nim said, but her father didn't seem to care as much as she'd thought he would.

"I'm never leaving you alone a—" And then he stopped and couldn't say anything more.

Alex was coming down the hill.

"There's something I've got to tell you," said Nim.

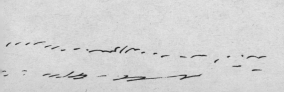

16

ALEX KNEW IT was unfair, but she hated Jack. She knew he hadn't meant to leave Nim alone for so long—but he had. She knew he hadn't wanted Nim to be lonely, worried, and frightened—but she had been.

She'd lain awake for an hour the night before, thinking of all the things she was going to say when she met him.

Then this lonely, exhausted man staggered in, looking as beaten as a Jack Russell who'd picked a fight with a Rottweiler. He sat and stared at his daughter, and Alex knew there was nothing she could say that was half as nasty as what he was saying to himself.

And when some of the shock had gone from his face, he looked too much like Nim for Alex to hate him.

"Who?" he said finally. "And how?"

"It's a long story," said Nim. "Tell us yours first: did the storm hit you?"

"Not the way it hit the island," Jack said, staring at the tumbles of shattered trees, "but fast enough that I hadn't put my life jacket and lifeline on yet, and strong enough to blow me overboard. The boat raced ahead; there was no land in sight . . . but floating in the current just ahead of me was a raft made of coconuts! What's so funny?"

Nim and Alex couldn't answer. They were laughing so hard that they fell over and rolled around on the ground like sea lion pups. "That's Alex's story!" Nim finally choked, and then they started from the beginning.

ALL THE NEXT WEEK, the three of them worked together: cleaning up the island, fishing and digging clams, collecting coconuts, and saving the garden. Every night they built a bonfire with the broken branches they'd cleaned up during the day, and Alex told them stories.

Nim listened hard so that she could remember the stories forever, after Alex left, and tried not to think about when that would happen.

But it wasn't Alex who talked first about leaving.

"When are we going to build a new hut?" Nim asked one morning, when the island was starting to look like her home again, just with not so many trees.

"Maybe we shouldn't," Jack said. "It's time I stopped being so selfish. Maybe we should go back to civilization so you can have a normal life."

"This *is* my normal life!" Nim shouted. "It's the one I want!"

She ran down the hill to Selkie, who left the king and

snuggled comfortingly around her. Fred curled across her shoulders.

Alex and Jack went for a walk in the other direction, around the point to Turtle Beach.

"They're talking about what's going to happen," Nim told her friends. "But if Jack makes me leave the island, I'll run away and live here with you like I did before!

"Jack only wants to go because he thinks that's what a good father should do, but I don't want a good father—I just want Jack, and I know he wants to stay on the island as much as I do!"

She wasn't even going to wish the other part because it was too much to hope for.

The morning changed to noon; the rock got hot; Selkie, Nim, and Fred went for a swim, climbed out to dry, and went for a quicker swim; and still Alex and Jack hadn't come back. Nim was hungry but the knots in her stomach were too tight for food.

The king barked for Selkie. Selkie looked miserable, and then she looked confused.

"You can go," Nim said. "I'm okay."

Selkie snuggled beside her a moment longer, but when the king barked again, she slid off the rock and into the sea.

Fred scuttled off to find some seaweed.

Alex and Jack came around the point and waded in the shallow water across to Nim.

They were smiling.

To: delia.defoe@papyrus.publishing.com
From: jack.rusoe@explorer.net
Date: Wednesday 21 April, 15:00
Subject: Really, this is Alex Rover
Dear Delia,

I have a small favor to ask you.

All right, it's small like a giant squid, and you might think it's about as easy to handle, but when I tell you the whole story and why I'm writing it on a borrowed Internet address (on a borrowed computer, wearing my new banana-leaf dress), you'll not only understand why I need a favor, you'll have a brand-new book. I promise you'll love it.

So...could you please go to my flat and pack up all my clothes, books, papers, and anything else you think would be useful on a small tropical island?

I'm attaching a shopping list. You'll need to find a good gardening and hardware store and a marine or boat suppliers as well as a department and grocery store.

The second attachment is a map. Please send the parcels by supply ship, parachute-drop, or helicopter, whichever works out best. You can take the cost out of the huge amount of money you'll want to pay me for this next book.

Yours, Alex

WENDY ORR *lives in the hills by the sea in southern Australia with her dog and other family. She was born in Canada and grew up with various pets, in various places across North America and France. Once, when her family sailed to a new home, the dogs wore life jackets, but the guinea pigs had to stay in their cages.*

Wendy is the author of several award-winning books for young children and teenagers.

KERRY MILLARD *was born in Canada and grew up surrounded by all sorts of animals, including a monkey. Later she moved to Australia and became a vet. One day Kerry took her crazy dog to dog school, drew some cartoons for the school's newsletter, and accidentally began a new career as an award-winning cartoonist, illustrator, and author.*